Sir Arthur Conan Doyle

THE HOUND OF THE BASKERVILLES

CAMPFIRE™

KALYANI NAVYUG MEDIA PVT LTD
NEW DELHI

2009001285

Sitting around the Campfire, telling the story, were:

Wordsmith	:	J. R. Parks
Illustrator	:	Vinod Kumar
Illustrations Editor	:	Jayshree Das
Colorist	:	Vijay Sharma
Letterers	:	Laxmi Chand Gupta
		Vishal Sharma
Editors	:	Eman Chowdhary
		Andrew Dodd
Editor (Informative Content)	:	Pushpanjali Borooah
Production Controller	:	Vishal Sharma

Cover Artists:

Illustrator	:	Vinod Kumar
Colorist	:	Anil C. K.
Designer	:	Manishi Gupta

Published by Kalyani Navyug Media Pvt Ltd
101 C, Shiv House, Hari Nagar Ashram
New Delhi 110014
India
www.campfire.co.in

ISBN: 978-93-80028-44-6

Printed in India at Rave India

About the Author

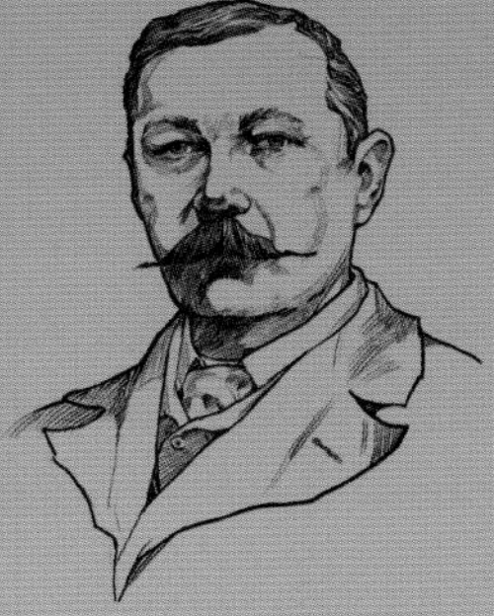

Sir Arthur Conan Doyle was born on May 22, 1859 in Edinburgh, Scotland, and is best known for his tales of the magnificent Sherlock Holmes.

Conan Doyle was born into a wealthy Christian family who were renowned in the art world. When he was nine years old, he was sent to a Roman Catholic Jesuit boarding school in England. However, he hated this school, and the cruel corporal punishment he was forced to endure.

During his years at boarding school, Conan Doyle found comfort and enjoyment from sending regular letters to his mother. This, along with the discovery that other students loved to hear him telling stories, was enough to convince him that he was a naturally talented writer and narrator.

While studying medicine at the University of Edinburgh, Conan Doyle was greatly impressed by one of his teachers, Dr. Joseph Bell. Dr. Bell was known for his powers of deduction and for the great ability to apply logic to a situation. Interestingly, Conan Doyle's most famous creation, Sherlock Holmes, shared many of the same characteristics as Dr. Bell and was, no doubt, greatly influenced by him.

On leaving university, Conan Doyle worked as a doctor in an independent practice. *A Study in Scarlet* was published in 1887, and was the first novel in which the characters of Sherlock Holmes and Dr. Watson were used. Following a severe bout of influenza in 1891, Conan Doyle decided to leave the medical profession in favor of his literary career. In hindsight, this was a prudent decision, as he went on to produce many more successful pieces of literature, including *The Hound of the Baskervilles.*

Sir Arthur Conan Doyle died in July 1930, at the age of seventy-one. His stories have entertained generations of readers for more than a century and will continue to do so for many more years to come.

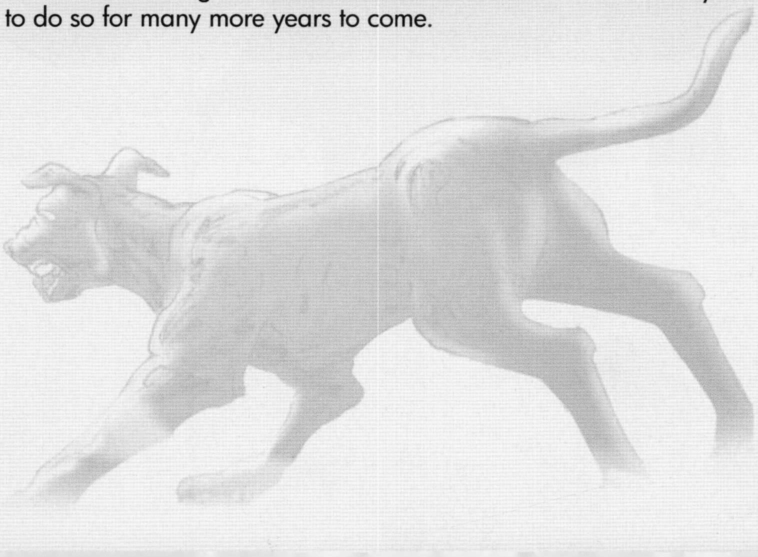

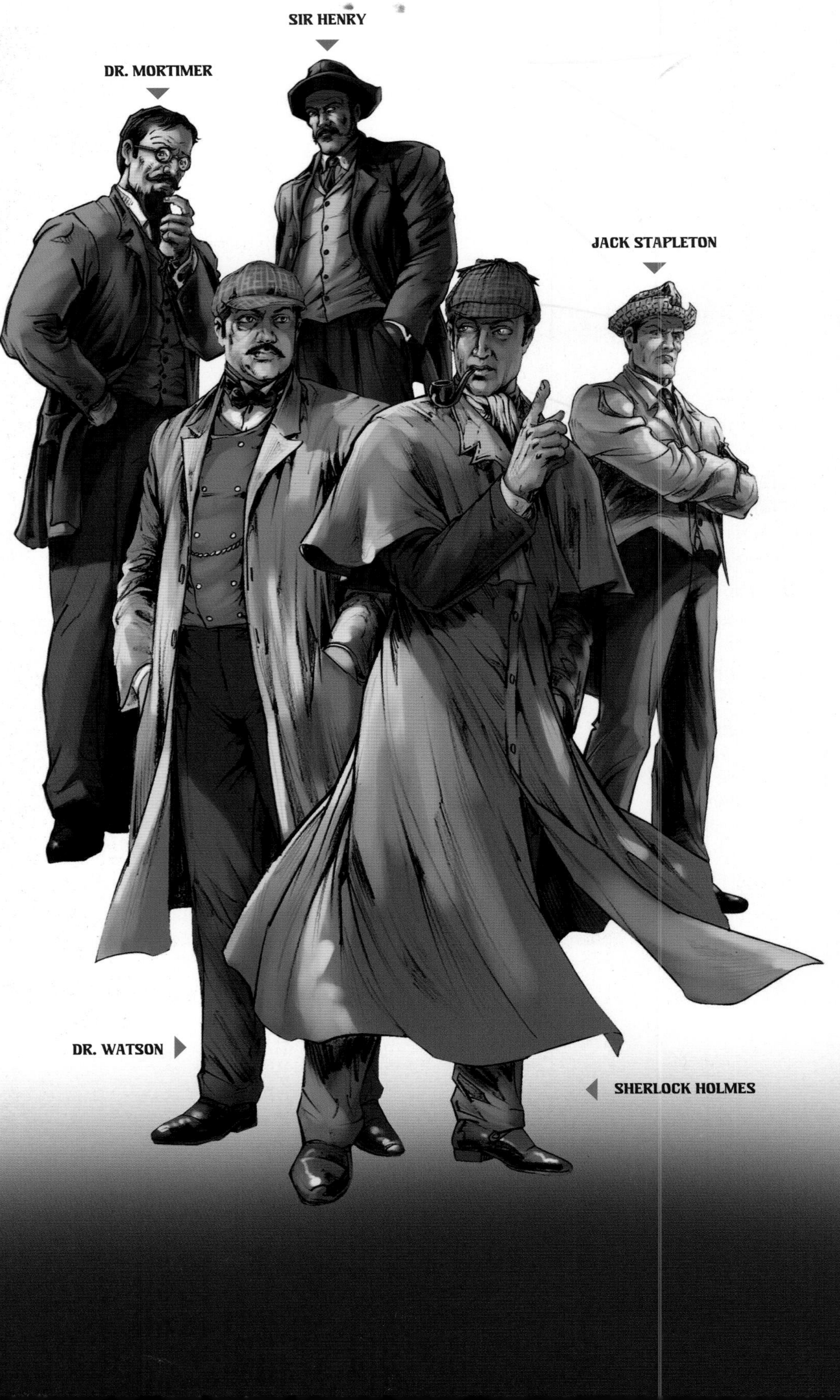
SIR HENRY
DR. MORTIMER
JACK STAPLETON
DR. WATSON
SHERLOCK HOLMES

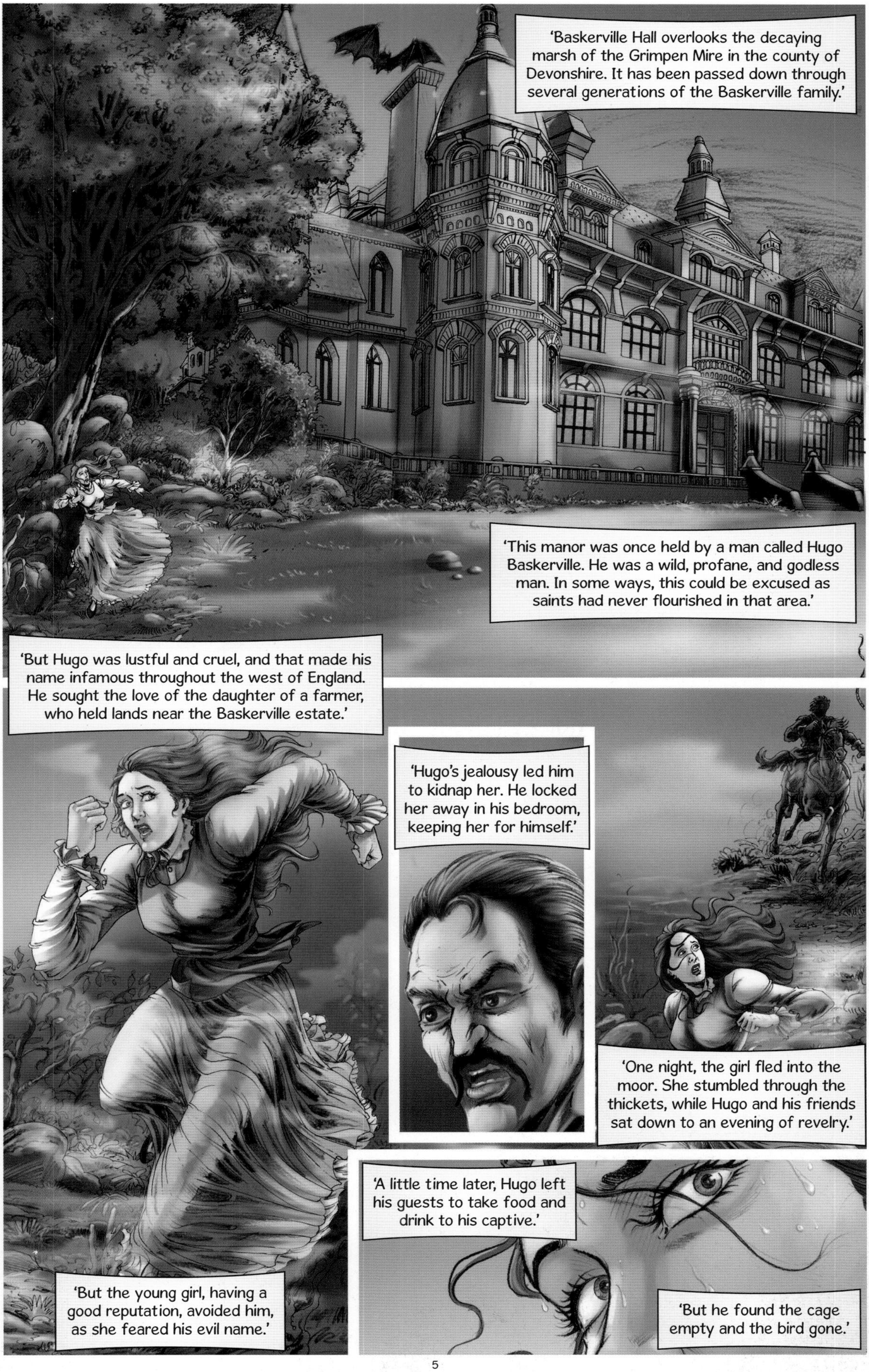
'Baskerville Hall overlooks the decaying marsh of the Grimpen Mire in the county of Devonshire. It has been passed down through several generations of the Baskerville family.'
'This manor was once held by a man called Hugo Baskerville. He was a wild, profane, and godless man. In some ways, this could be excused as saints had never flourished in that area.'
'But Hugo was lustful and cruel, and that made his name infamous throughout the west of England. He sought the love of the daughter of a farmer, who held lands near the Baskerville estate.'
'But the young girl, having a good reputation, avoided him, as she feared his evil name.'
'Hugo's jealousy led him to kidnap her. He locked her away in his bedroom, keeping her for himself.'
'One night, the girl fled into the moor. She stumbled through the thickets, while Hugo and his friends sat down to an evening of revelry.'
'A little time later, Hugo left his guests to take food and drink to his captive.'
'But he found the cage empty and the bird gone.'

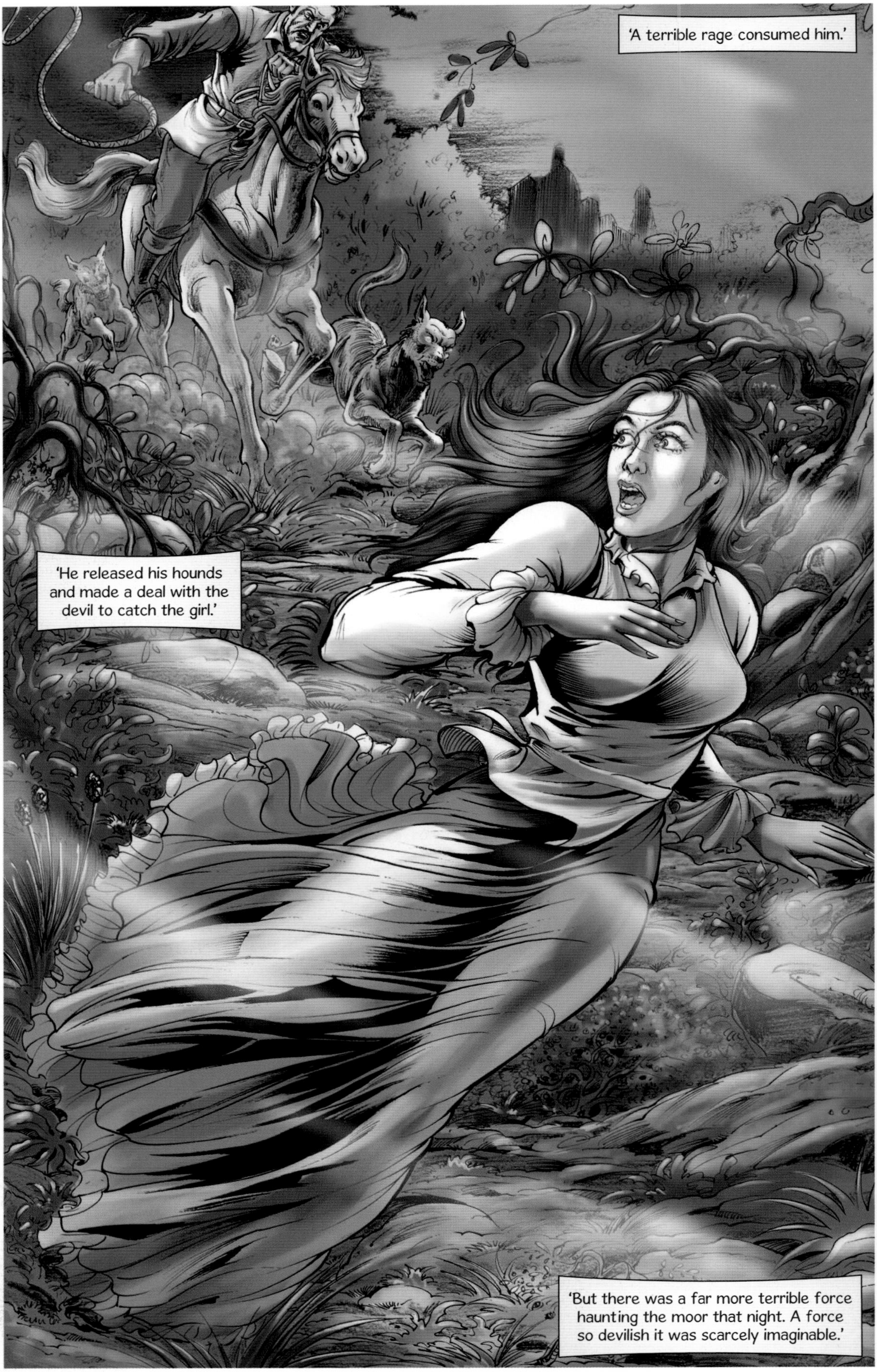
'A terrible rage consumed him.'
'He released his hounds and made a deal with the devil to catch the girl.'
'But there was a far more terrible force haunting the moor that night. A force so devilish it was scarcely imaginable.'

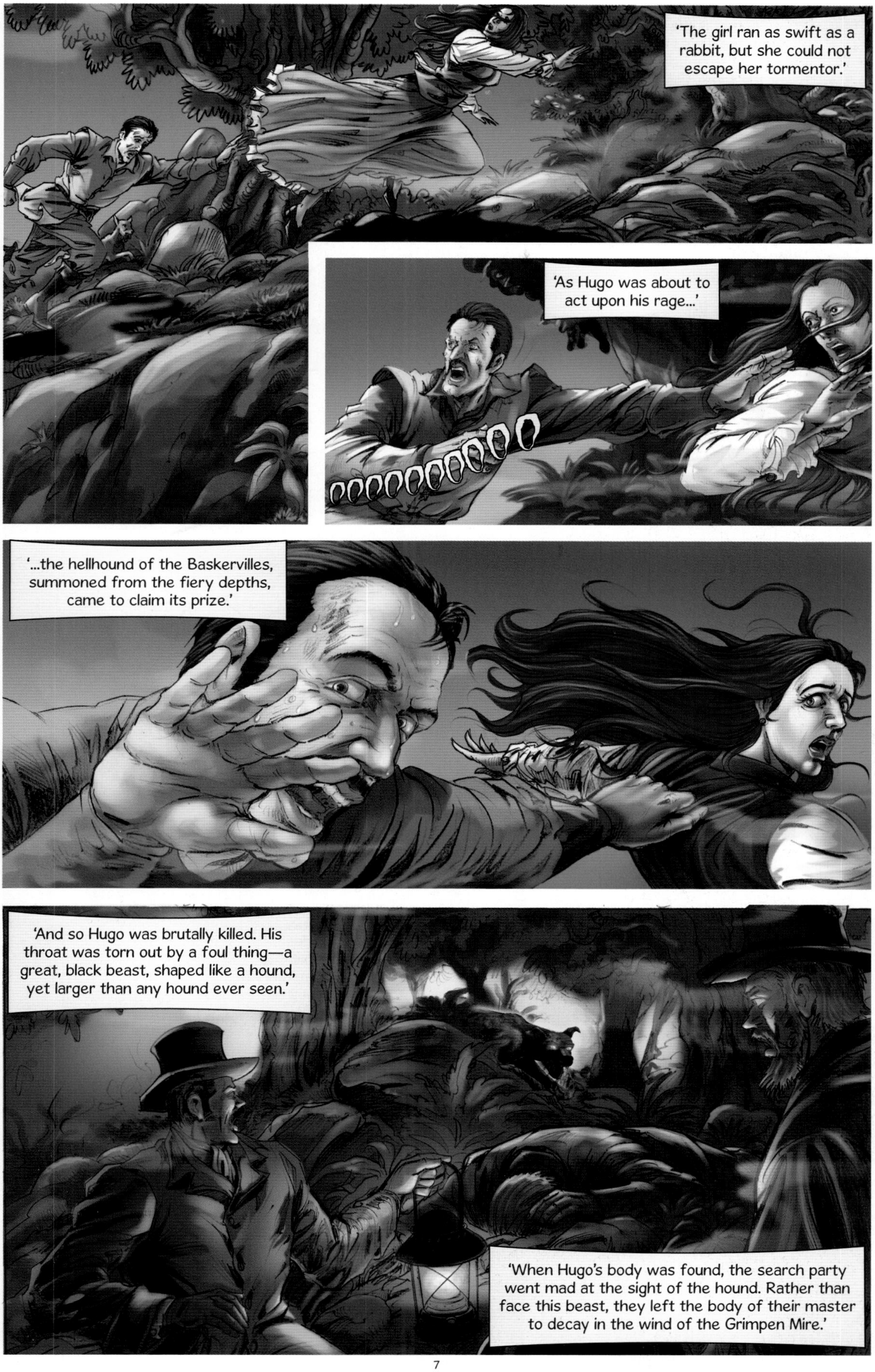
'The girl ran as swift as a rabbit, but she could not escape her tormentor.'
'As Hugo was about to act upon his rage...'
'...the hellhound of the Baskervilles, summoned from the fiery depths, came to claim its prize.'
'And so Hugo was brutally killed. His throat was torn out by a foul thing—a great, black beast, shaped like a hound, yet larger than any hound ever seen.'
'When Hugo's body was found, the search party went mad at the sight of the hound. Rather than face this beast, they left the body of their master to decay in the wind of the Grimpen Mire.'

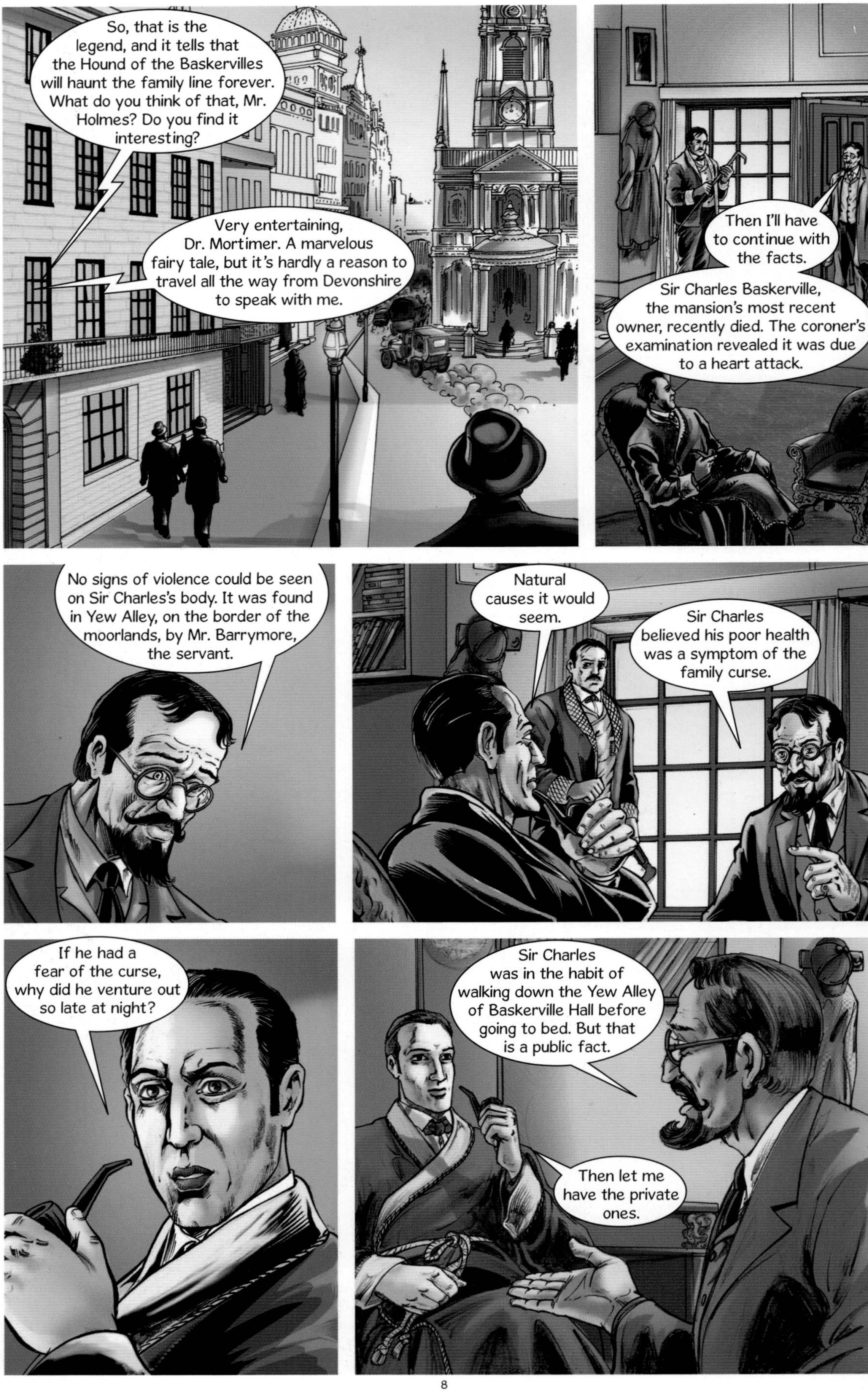
So, that is the legend, and it tells that the Hound of the Baskervilles will haunt the family line forever. What do you think of that, Mr. Holmes? Do you find it interesting?
Very entertaining, Dr. Mortimer. A marvelous fairy tale, but it's hardly a reason to travel all the way from Devonshire to speak with me.
Then I'll have to continue with the facts.
Sir Charles Baskerville, the mansion's most recent owner, recently died. The coroner's examination revealed it was due to a heart attack.
No signs of violence could be seen on Sir Charles's body. It was found in Yew Alley, on the border of the moorlands, by Mr. Barrymore, the servant.
Natural causes it would seem.
Sir Charles believed his poor health was a symptom of the family curse.
If he had a fear of the curse, why did he venture out so late at night?
Sir Charles was in the habit of walking down the Yew Alley of Baskerville Hall before going to bed. But that is a public fact.
Then let me have the private ones.

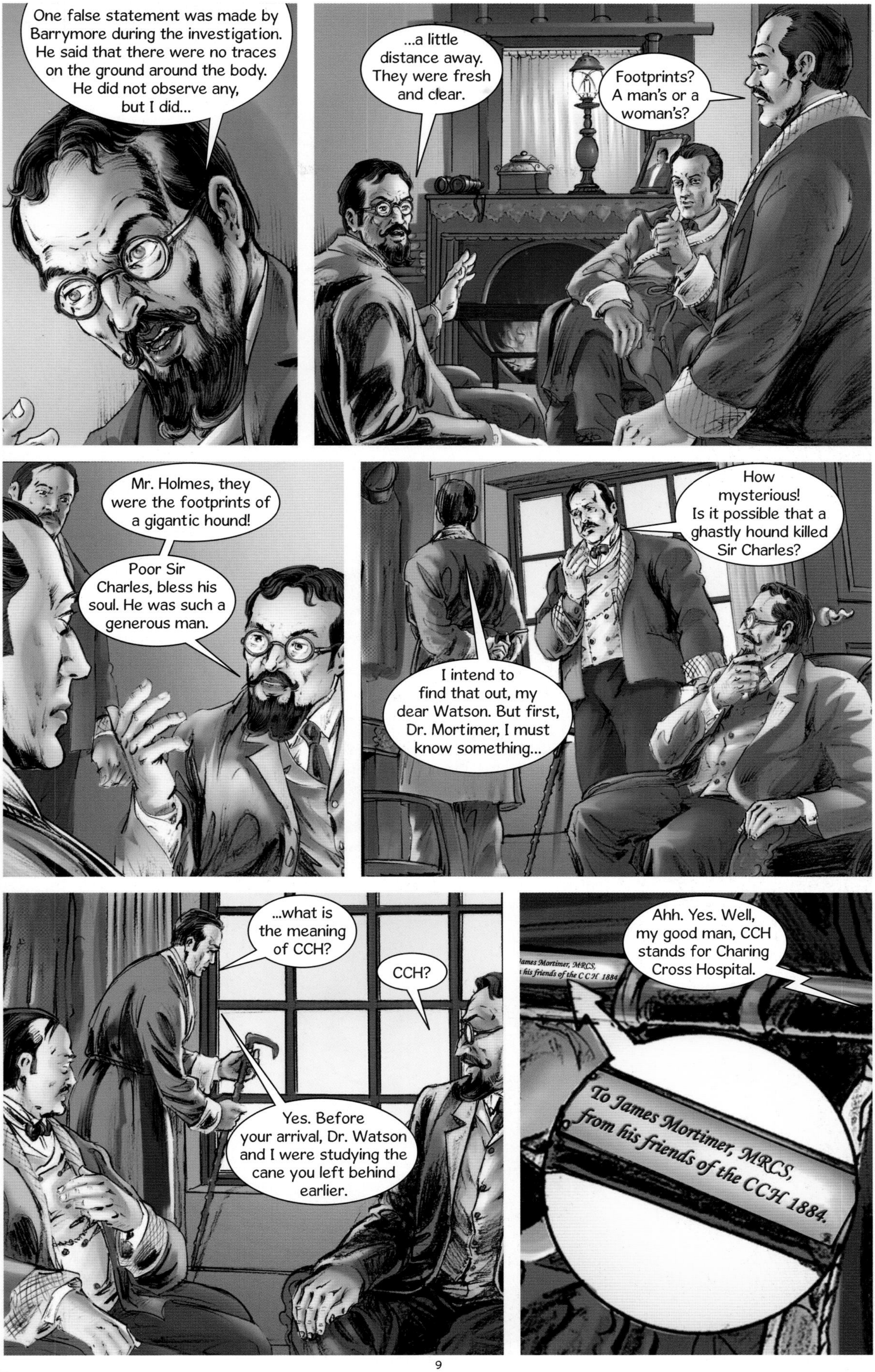
One false statement was made by Barrymore during the investigation. He said that there were no traces on the ground around the body. He did not observe any, but I did...
...a little distance away. They were fresh and clear.
Footprints? A man's or a woman's?
Mr. Holmes, they were the footprints of a gigantic hound!
Poor Sir Charles, bless his soul. He was such a generous man.
How mysterious! Is it possible that a ghastly hound killed Sir Charles?
I intend to find that out, my dear Watson. But first, Dr. Mortimer, I must know something...
...what is the meaning of CCH?
CCH?
Yes. Before your arrival, Dr. Watson and I were studying the cane you left behind earlier.
Ahh. Yes. Well, my good man, CCH stands for Charing Cross Hospital.
To James Mortimer, MRCS, from his friends of the CCH 1884.

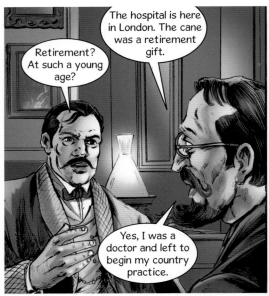

Retirement? At such a young age?

The hospital is here in London. The cane was a retirement gift.

Yes, I was a doctor and left to begin my country practice.

See, Watson, you were right about one thing—he does indeed live in the country.

Yes, but you knew what CCH meant even before Dr. Mortimer mentioned it. And you knew he was retired. How did you work all that out?

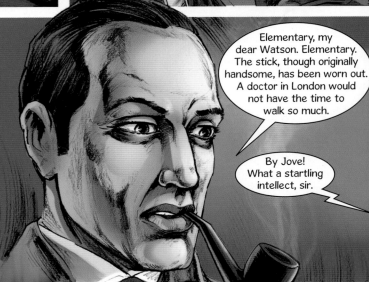

Elementary, my dear Watson. Elementary. The stick, though originally handsome, has been worn out. A doctor in London would not have the time to walk so much.

By Jove! What a startling intellect, sir.

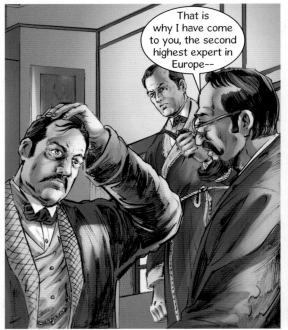

That is why I have come to you, the second highest expert in Europe--

Indeed, sir! May I inquire who has the honor of being the first?

Monsieur Bertillon, to the scientific mind. But, as a practical man of affairs, it is acknowledged that you stand alone.

That is why I brought you this old manuscript. It was given to me by Sir Charles Baskerville, three months before his sudden death.

May I see it?

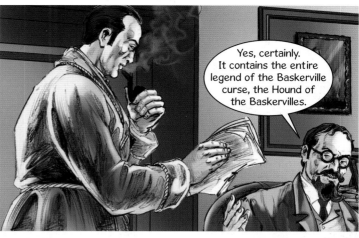

Yes, certainly. It contains the entire legend of the Baskerville curse, the Hound of the Baskervilles.

It all began during the time of the Great Rebellion with the story of the wicked and cruel Hugo Baskerville, as I told you earlier.

If I'm to help you, I must know everything, Dr. Mortimer.

I have discovered that, before the event occurred, several people saw a creature on the moors that corresponds with the Baskerville demon. They all agreed that it was a huge creature—luminous, ghastly, and spectral.

Yew Alley is surrounded by gates, which means the hound never came near Charles. Therefore, the beast must have used supernatural powers to kill him.

Now, now. We mustn't jump to conclusions. There are other things to consider.

Things to consider, indeed! Sir Henry Baskerville, Charles's nephew and sole heir to the estate, arrives at Waterloo Station in exactly one hour and fifteen minutes.

I came here to ask for your advice, as I fear for his safety. He's returning to Devonshire to continue his uncle's good work.

Well, this is a lot to think about. I will need time alone, gentlemen. Do bring Sir Henry to see me in the morning, Dr. Mortimer. There is a lot to discuss with him.

I knew that seclusion and solitude were necessary for my friend in those hours of intense mental concentration. I, therefore, spent the rest of the day at my club and returned to Baker Street in the evening.

Have you caught a cold, Watson?

No, it's this poisonous atmosphere.

Open the window then.

COUGH COUGH

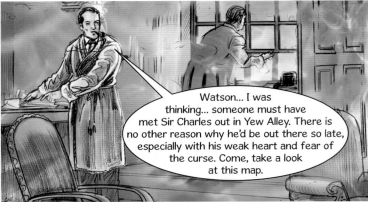

Watson... I was thinking... someone must have met Sir Charles out in Yew Alley. There is no other reason why he'd be out there so late, especially with his weak heart and fear of the curse. Come, take a look at this map.

But who, Holmes?

I'm not sure yet, Watson, but someone met him there. Someone who knows what happened the night Sir Charles Baskerville died.

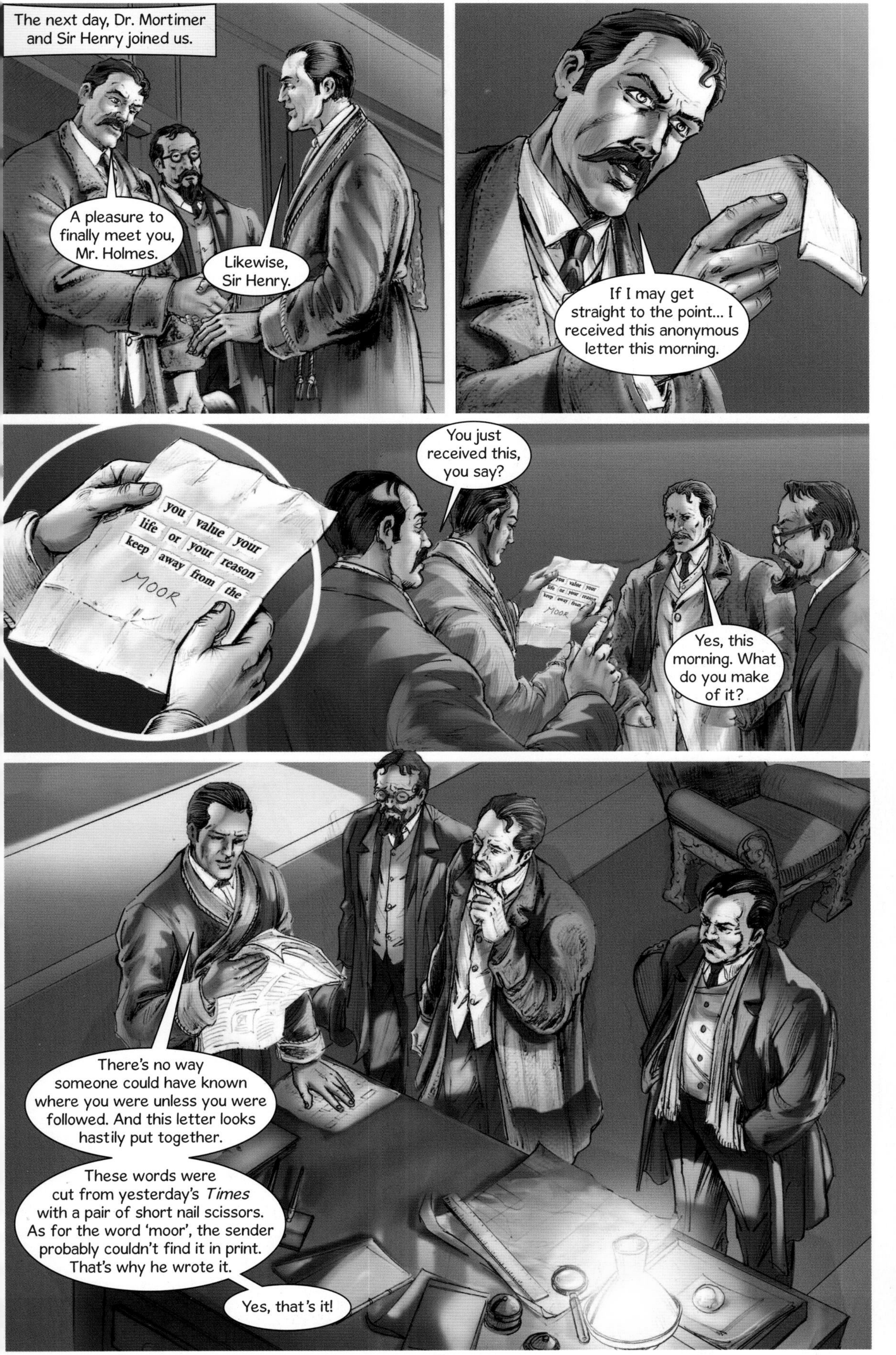

The next day, Dr. Mortimer and Sir Henry joined us.
A pleasure to finally meet you, Mr. Holmes.
Likewise, Sir Henry.
If I may get straight to the point... I received this anonymous letter this morning.
you value your life or your reason keep away from the MOOR
You just received this, you say?
Yes, this morning. What do you make of it?
There's no way someone could have known where you were unless you were followed. And this letter looks hastily put together.
These words were cut from yesterday's *Times* with a pair of short nail scissors. As for the word 'moor', the sender probably couldn't find it in print. That's why he wrote it.
Yes, that's it!

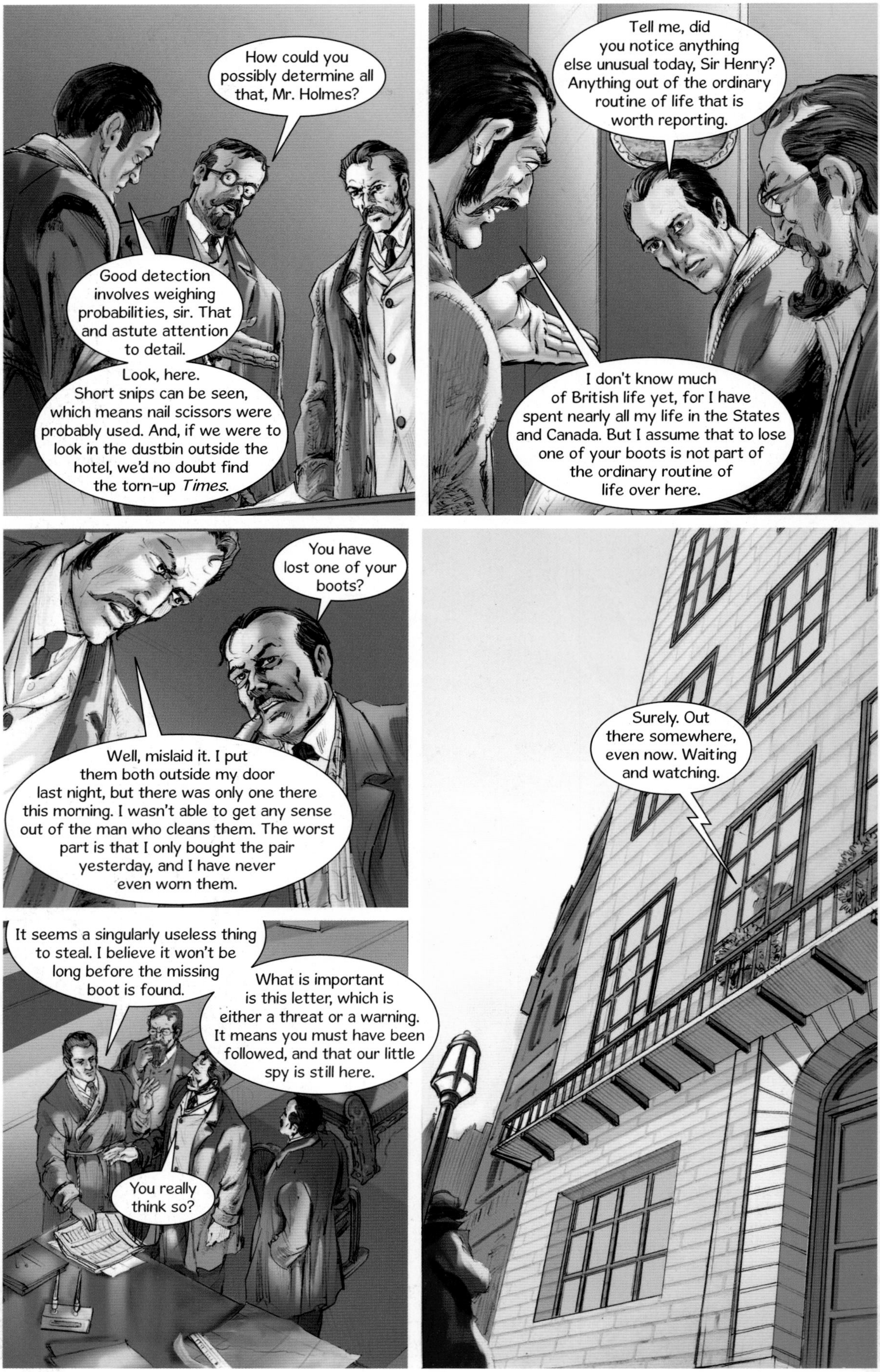
How could you possibly determine all that, Mr. Holmes?
Good detection involves weighing probabilities, sir. That and astute attention to detail.
Look, here. Short snips can be seen, which means nail scissors were probably used. And, if we were to look in the dustbin outside the hotel, we'd no doubt find the torn-up *Times*.
Tell me, did you notice anything else unusual today, Sir Henry? Anything out of the ordinary routine of life that is worth reporting.
I don't know much of British life yet, for I have spent nearly all my life in the States and Canada. But I assume that to lose one of your boots is not part of the ordinary routine of life over here.
You have lost one of your boots?
Well, mislaid it. I put them both outside my door last night, but there was only one there this morning. I wasn't able to get any sense out of the man who cleans them. The worst part is that I only bought the pair yesterday, and I have never even worn them.
It seems a singularly useless thing to steal. I believe it won't be long before the missing boot is found.
What is important is this letter, which is either a threat or a warning. It means you must have been followed, and that our little spy is still here.
You really think so?
Surely. Out there somewhere, even now. Waiting and watching.

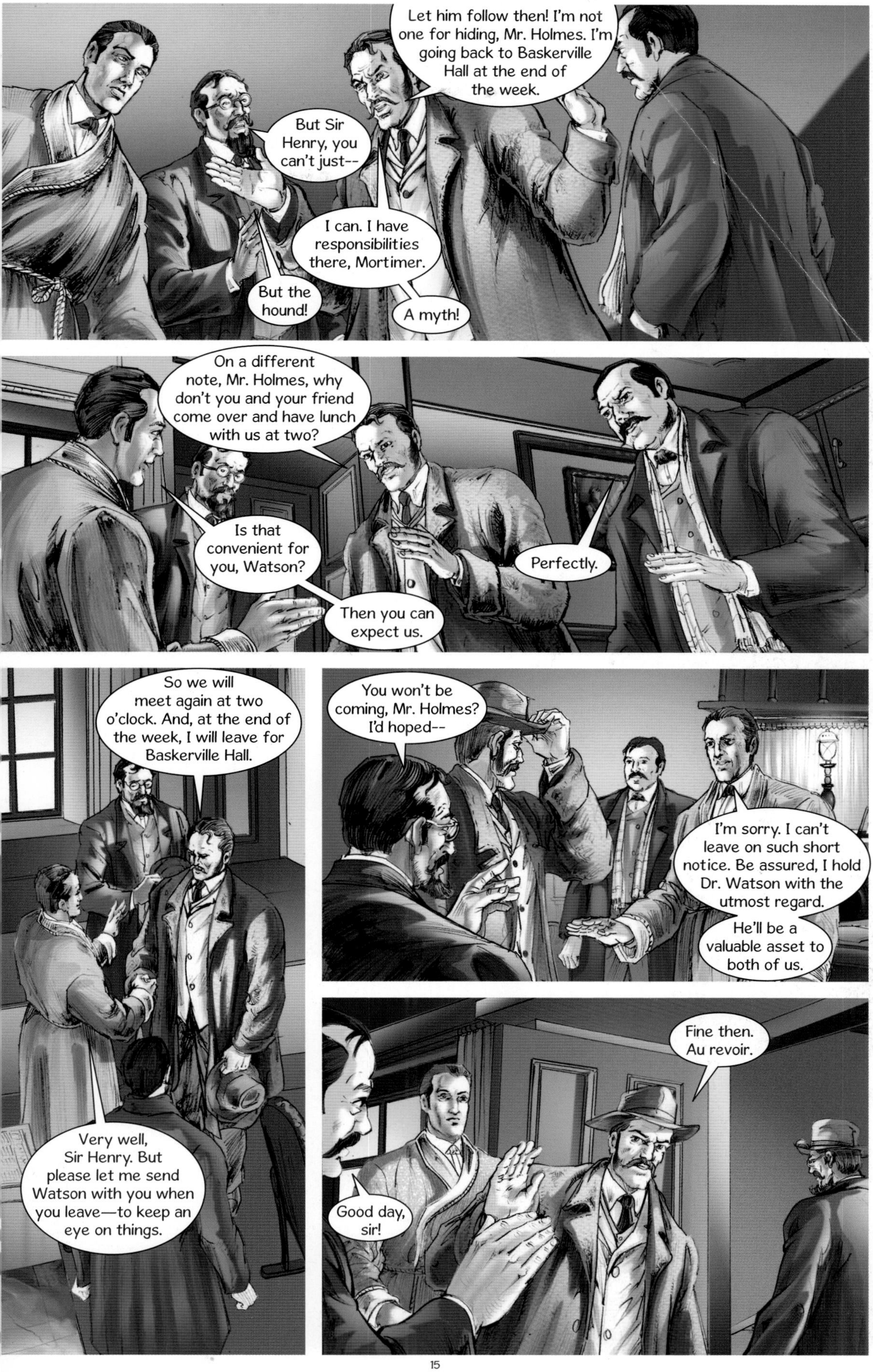
Let him follow then! I'm not one for hiding, Mr. Holmes. I'm going back to Baskerville Hall at the end of the week.
But Sir Henry, you can't just--
I can. I have responsibilities there, Mortimer.
But the hound!
A myth!
On a different note, Mr. Holmes, why don't you and your friend come over and have lunch with us at two?
Is that convenient for you, Watson?
Perfectly.
Then you can expect us.
So we will meet again at two o'clock. And, at the end of the week, I will leave for Baskerville Hall.
Very well, Sir Henry. But please let me send Watson with you when you leave—to keep an eye on things.
You won't be coming, Mr. Holmes? I'd hoped--
I'm sorry. I can't leave on such short notice. Be assured, I hold Dr. Watson with the utmost regard.
He'll be a valuable asset to both of us.
Fine then. Au revoir.
Good day, sir!

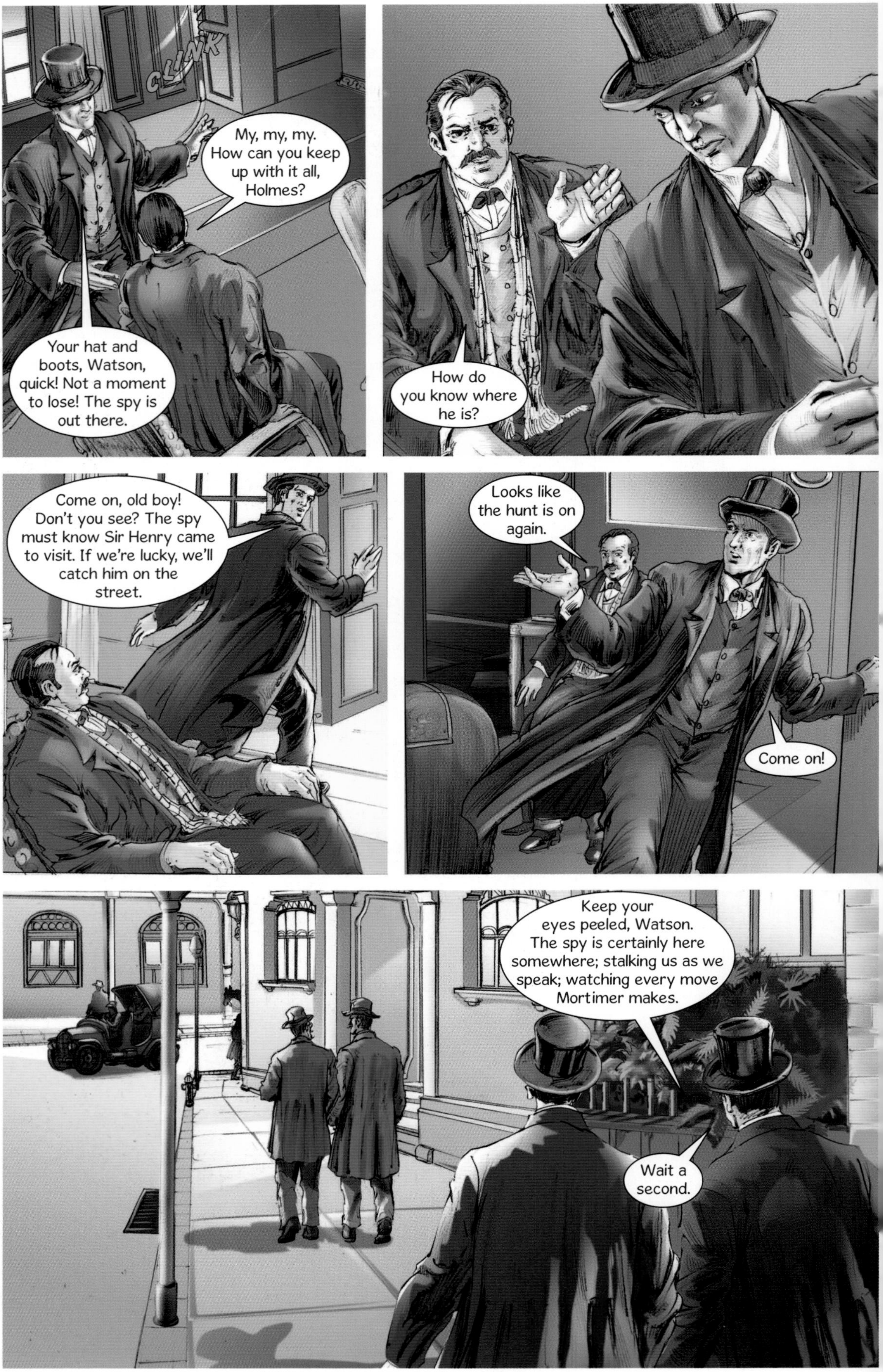
CLINK
My, my, my. How can you keep up with it all, Holmes?
Your hat and boots, Watson, quick! Not a moment to lose! The spy is out there.
How do you know where he is?
Come on, old boy! Don't you see? The spy must know Sir Henry came to visit. If we're lucky, we'll catch him on the street.
Looks like the hunt is on again.
Come on!
Keep your eyes peeled, Watson. The spy is certainly here somewhere; stalking us as we speak; watching every move Mortimer makes.
Wait a second.

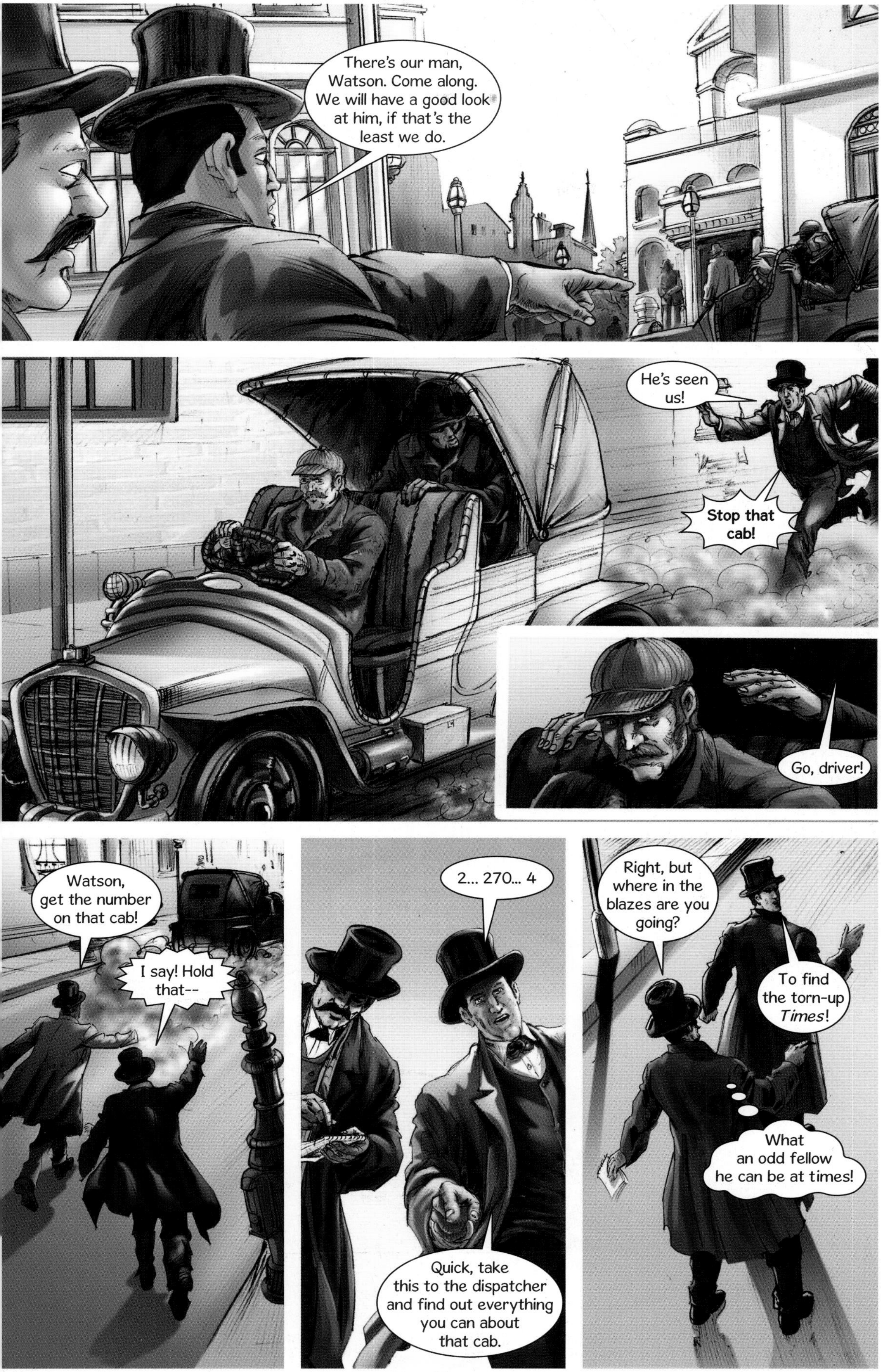
There's our man, Watson. Come along. We will have a good look at him, if that's the least we do.
He's seen us!
Stop that cab!
Go, driver!
Watson, get the number on that cab!
I say! Hold that--
2... 270... 4
Quick, take this to the dispatcher and find out everything you can about that cab.
Right, but where in the blazes are you going?
To find the torn-up *Times*!
What an odd fellow he can be at times!

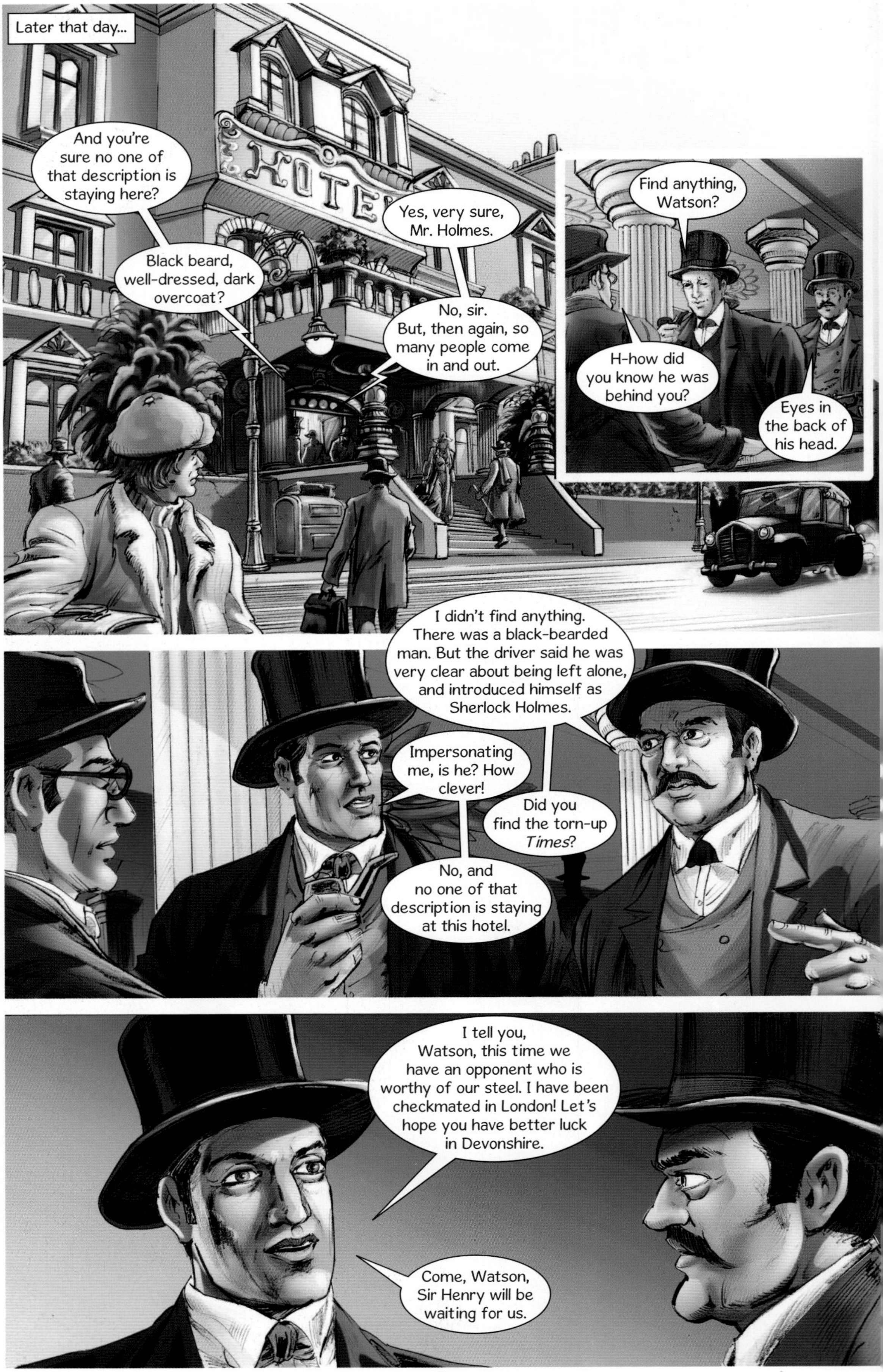
Later that day...
And you're sure no one of that description is staying here?
Yes, very sure, Mr. Holmes.
Black beard, well-dressed, dark overcoat?
No, sir. But, then again, so many people come in and out.
Find anything, Watson?
H-how did you know he was behind you?
Eyes in the back of his head.
I didn't find anything. There was a black-bearded man. But the driver said he was very clear about being left alone, and introduced himself as Sherlock Holmes.
Impersonating me, is he? How clever!
Did you find the torn-up *Times*?
No, and no one of that description is staying at this hotel.
I tell you, Watson, this time we have an opponent who is worthy of our steel. I have been checkmated in London! Let's hope you have better luck in Devonshire.
Come, Watson, Sir Henry will be waiting for us.

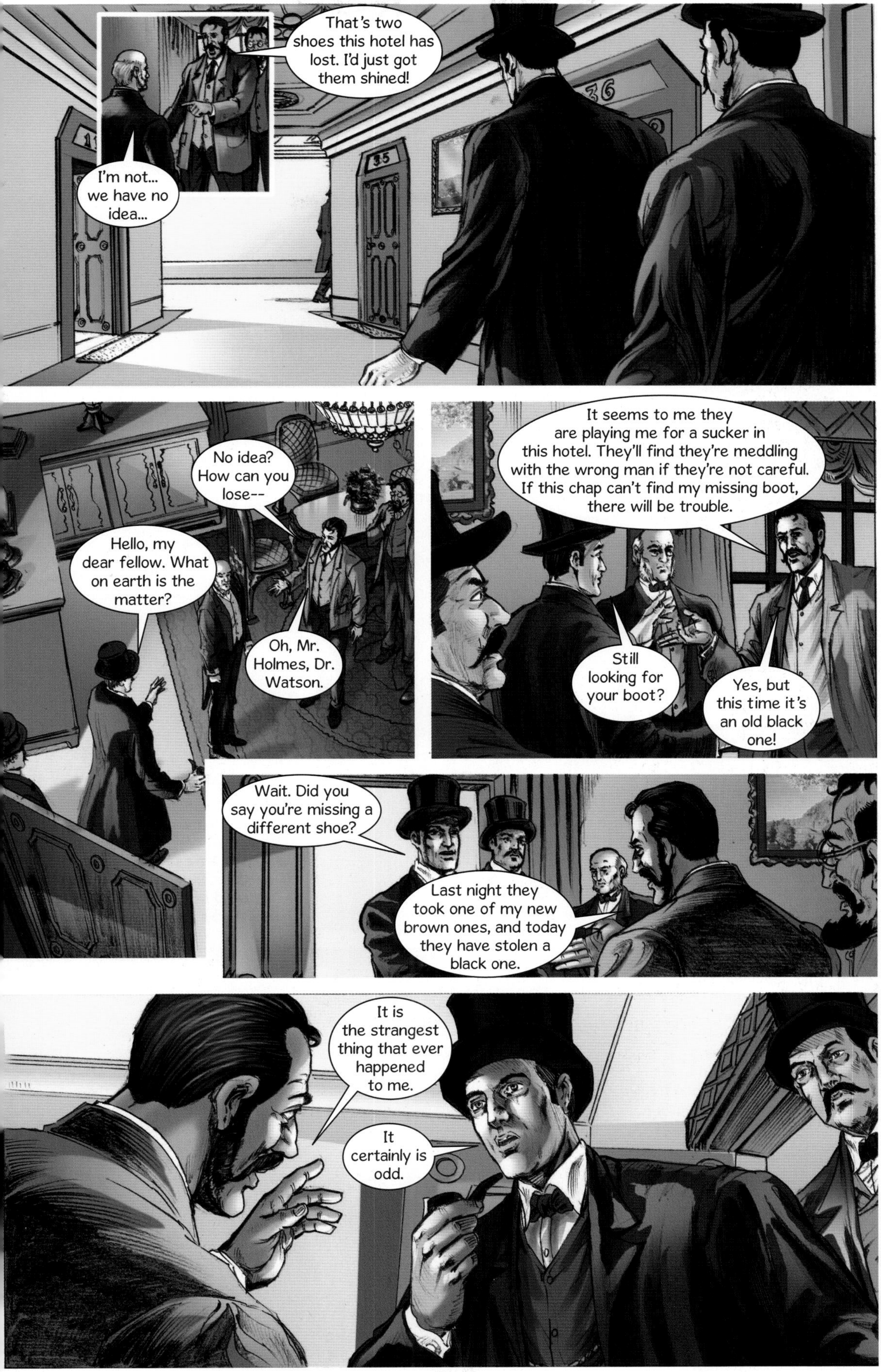
That's two shoes this hotel has lost. I'd just got them shined!
I'm not... we have no idea...
No idea? How can you lose--
Hello, my dear fellow. What on earth is the matter?
Oh, Mr. Holmes, Dr. Watson.
It seems to me they are playing me for a sucker in this hotel. They'll find they're meddling with the wrong man if they're not careful. If this chap can't find my missing boot, there will be trouble.
Still looking for your boot?
Yes, but this time it's an old black one!
Wait. Did you say you're missing a different shoe?
Last night they took one of my new brown ones, and today they have stolen a black one.
It is the strangest thing that ever happened to me.
It certainly is odd.

Didn't you know, Dr. Mortimer, that you were followed from my house this morning?

Followed! By whom?

That, unfortunately, is what I cannot tell you.

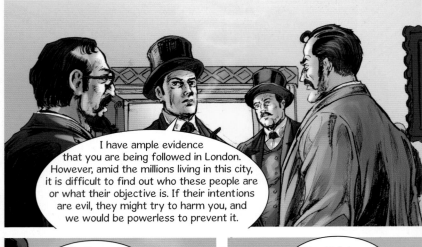

I have ample evidence that you are being followed in London. However, amid the millions living in this city, it is difficult to find out who these people are or what their objective is. If their intentions are evil, they might try to harm you, and we would be powerless to prevent it.

By the way, do you know anyone with a black beard by any chance?

Just Mr. Barrymore.

The butler back home in Baskerville Hall?

Yes. He's been with the family for a long time. He and his wife.

Does Mr. Barrymore stand to benefit from Charles's death?

Well, yes, to a degree. About five hundred pounds, and no more work for the household. But even I inherited a thousand pounds. Everything else, which is around seven hundred and forty thousand pounds, is left to Sir Henry.

My God! It is a stake that someone might play a desperate game for.

And supposing anything happened to our young friend here—please forgive the unpleasant hypothesis—who would inherit the estate?

Rodger Baskerville, Sir Charles's younger brother, died unmarried. Therefore, the estate would descend to the Desmonds, who are his distant cousins. James Desmond is an elderly clergyman in Westmoreland.

Thank you. These details are of great interest.

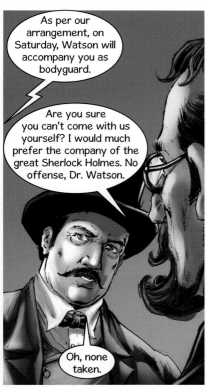

As per our arrangement, on Saturday, Watson will accompany you as bodyguard.

Are you sure you can't come with us yourself? I would much prefer the company of the great Sherlock Holmes. No offense, Dr. Watson.

Oh, none taken.

Yes, I'm afraid I absolutely cannot follow you just yet. But please, trust my judgment. Dr. Watson is a fine man, and he'll have his gun, just in case you need it.

See you on Saturday then.

On Saturday morning...

PADDINGTON

To Baskerville Hall then?

Yes. Good day, Mr. Holmes. I hope we'll be seeing you shortly.

Of course, sir.

Watson, listen to me very carefully. Keep close watch on Sir Henry and Mr. Barrymore. And anyone else—local farmers, friends. Anyone.

I will certainly do my best, Holmes. I'll be an eagle in the sky.

You'll be more than that, old chum. You'll be my eyes, too. Take note of every detail. Just the facts, mind you; none of your own intuitions. Just the facts, Watson.

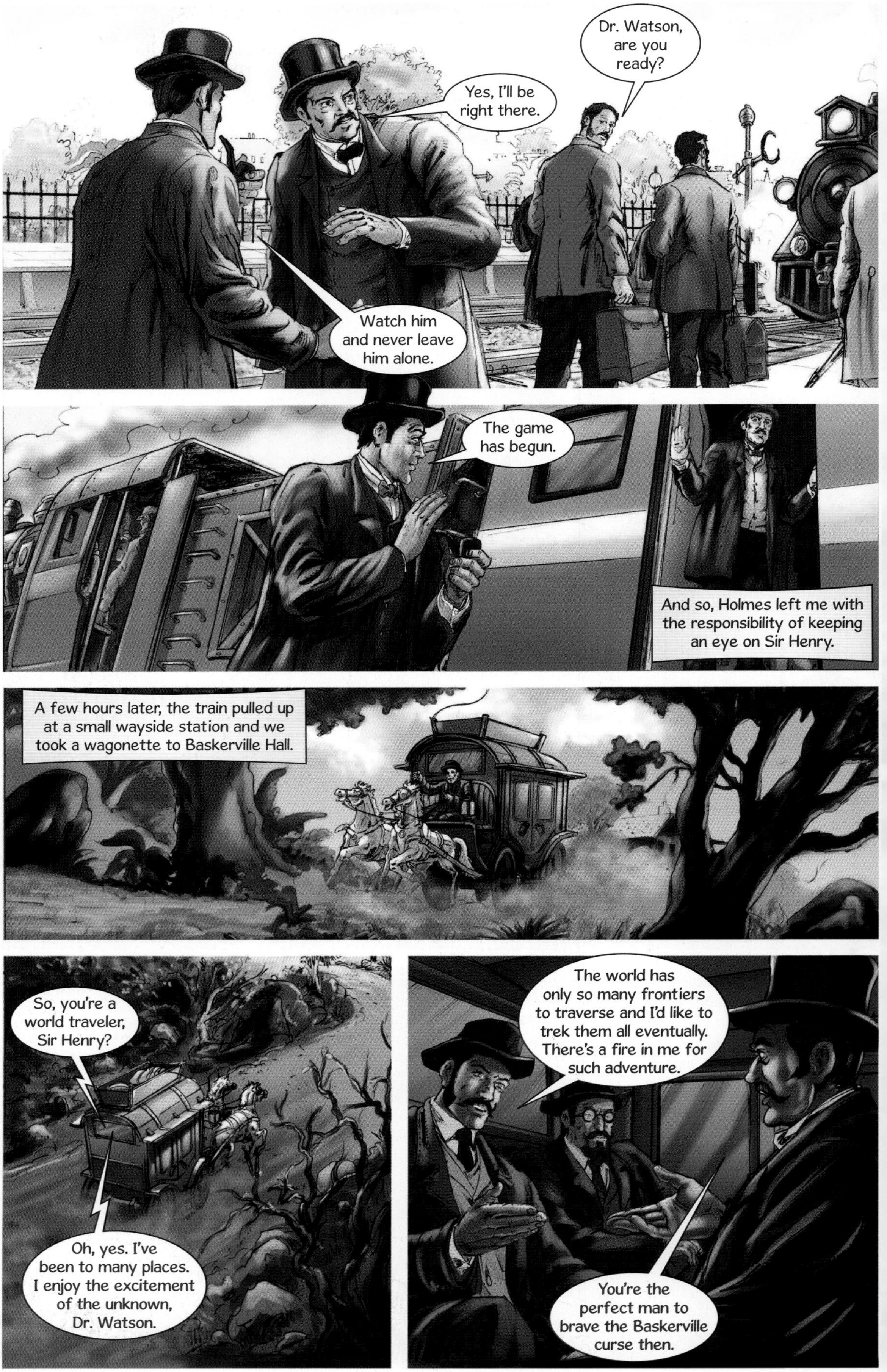
Dr. Watson, are you ready?
Yes, I'll be right there.
Watch him and never leave him alone.
The game has begun.
And so, Holmes left me with the responsibility of keeping an eye on Sir Henry.
A few hours later, the train pulled up at a small wayside station and we took a wagonette to Baskerville Hall.
So, you're a world traveler, Sir Henry?
Oh, yes. I've been to many places. I enjoy the excitement of the unknown, Dr. Watson.
The world has only so many frontiers to traverse and I'd like to trek them all eventually. There's a fire in me for such adventure.
You're the perfect man to brave the Baskerville curse then.

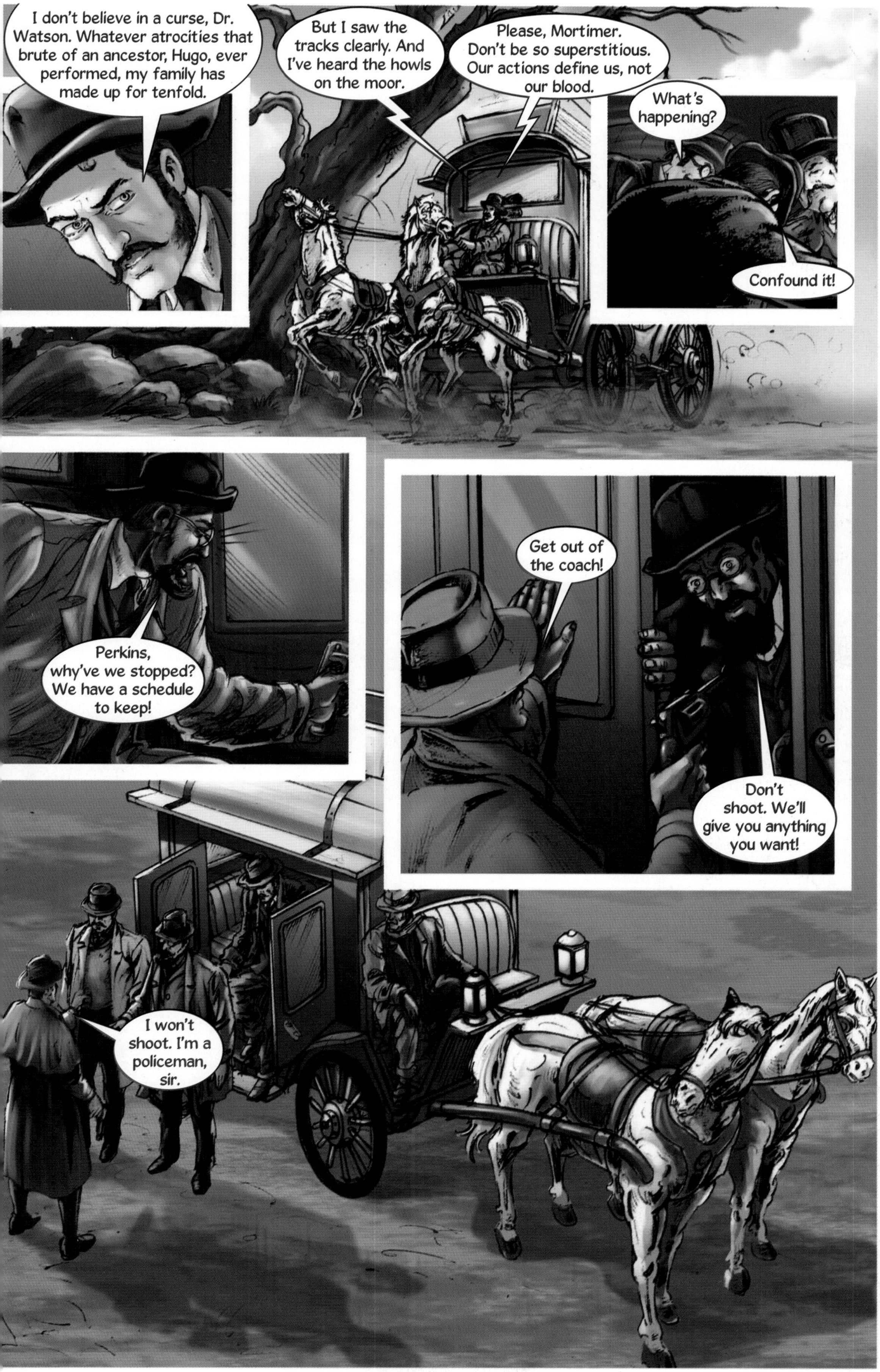
I don't believe in a curse, Dr. Watson. Whatever atrocities that brute of an ancestor, Hugo, ever performed, my family has made up for tenfold.
But I saw the tracks clearly. And I've heard the howls on the moor.
Please, Mortimer. Don't be so superstitious. Our actions define us, not our blood.
What's happening?
Confound it!
Perkins, why've we stopped? We have a schedule to keep!
Get out of the coach!
Don't shoot. We'll give you anything you want!
I won't shoot. I'm a policeman, sir.

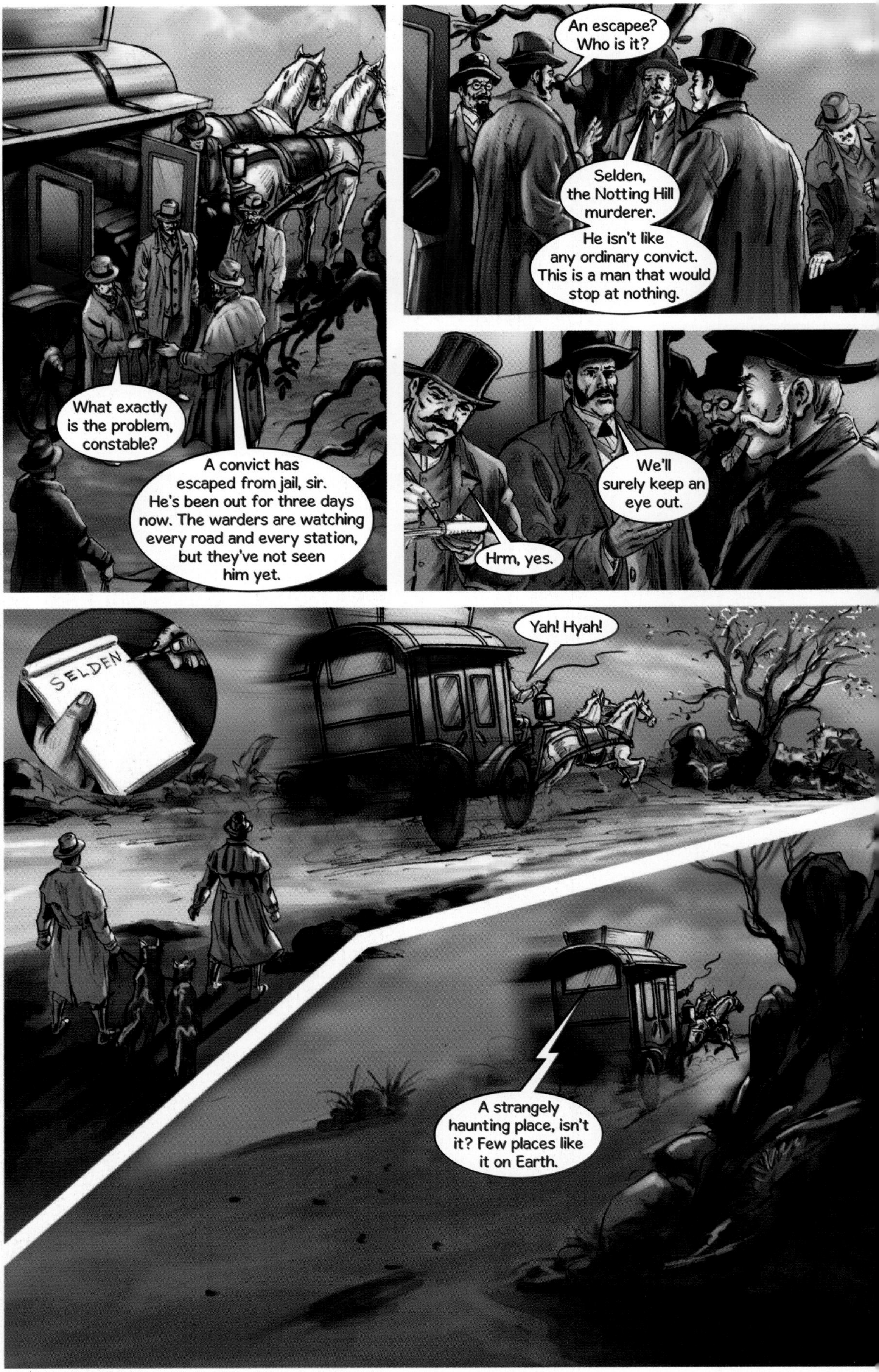
What exactly is the problem, constable?
A convict has escaped from jail, sir. He's been out for three days now. The warders are watching every road and every station, but they've not seen him yet.
An escapee? Who is it?
Selden, the Notting Hill murderer.
He isn't like any ordinary convict. This is a man that would stop at nothing.
We'll surely keep an eye out.
Hrm, yes.
SELDEN
Yah! Hyah!
A strangely haunting place, isn't it? Few places like it on Earth.

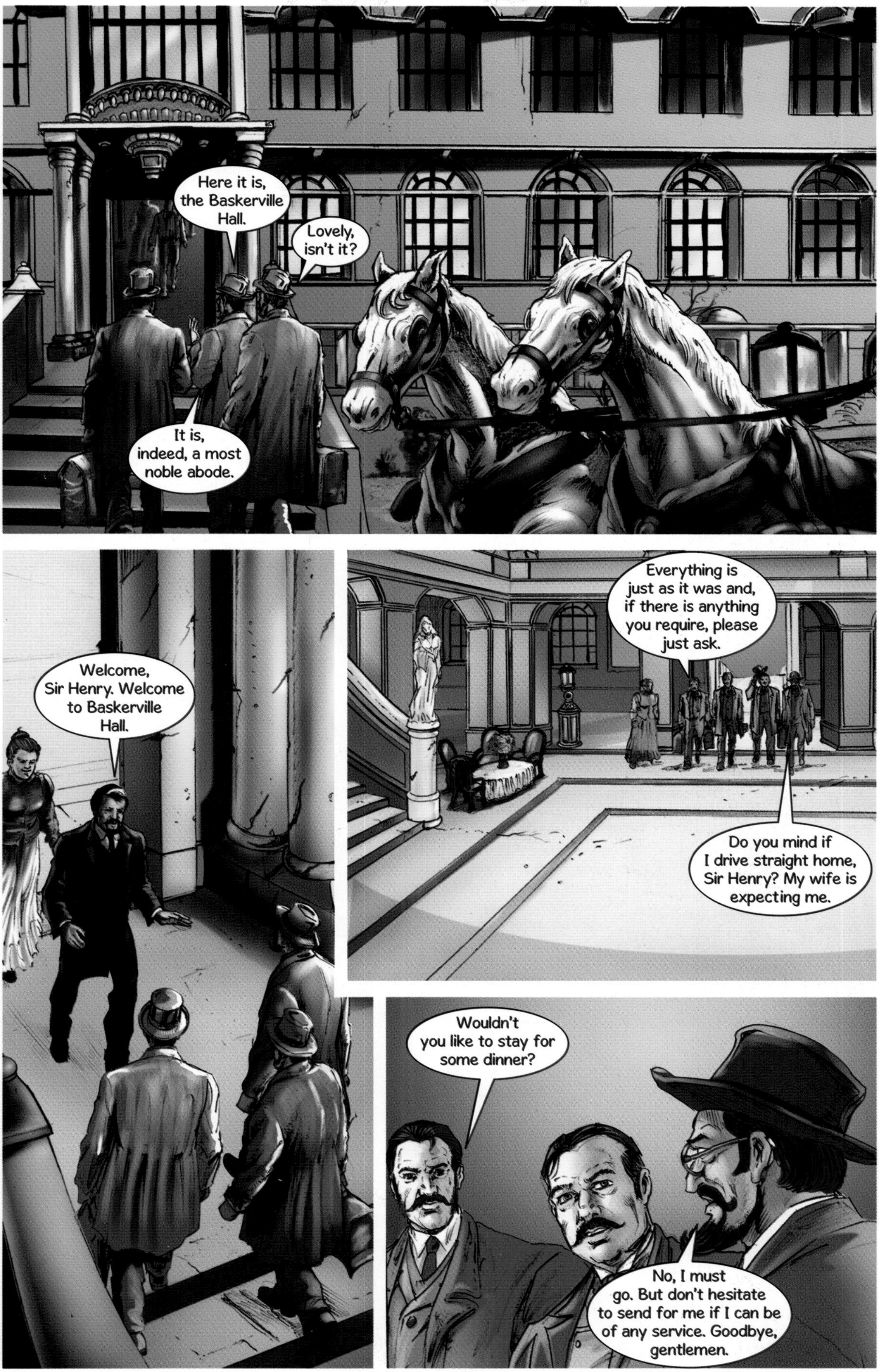

Here it is, the Baskerville Hall.
Lovely, isn't it?
It is, indeed, a most noble abode.
Welcome, Sir Henry. Welcome to Baskerville Hall.
Everything is just as it was and, if there is anything you require, please just ask.
Do you mind if I drive straight home, Sir Henry? My wife is expecting me.
Wouldn't you like to stay for some dinner?
No, I must go. But don't hesitate to send for me if I can be of any service. Goodbye, gentlemen.

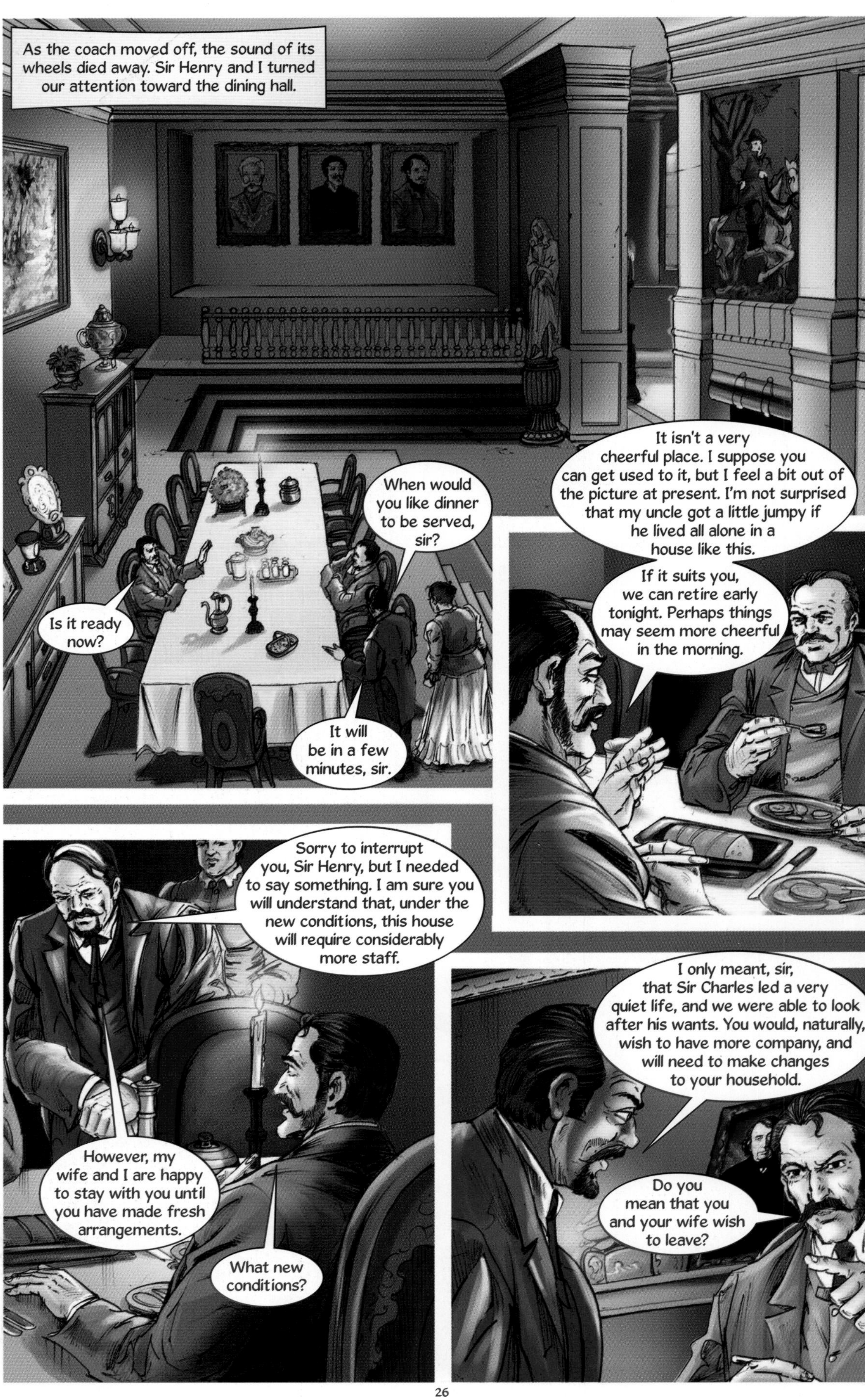
As the coach moved off, the sound of its wheels died away. Sir Henry and I turned our attention toward the dining hall.
When would you like dinner to be served, sir?
Is it ready now?
It will be in a few minutes, sir.
It isn't a very cheerful place. I suppose you can get used to it, but I feel a bit out of the picture at present. I'm not surprised that my uncle got a little jumpy if he lived all alone in a house like this.
If it suits you, we can retire early tonight. Perhaps things may seem more cheerful in the morning.
Sorry to interrupt you, Sir Henry, but I needed to say something. I am sure you will understand that, under the new conditions, this house will require considerably more staff.
However, my wife and I are happy to stay with you until you have made fresh arrangements.
What new conditions?
I only meant, sir, that Sir Charles led a very quiet life, and we were able to look after his wants. You would, naturally, wish to have more company, and will need to make changes to your household.
Do you mean that you and your wife wish to leave?

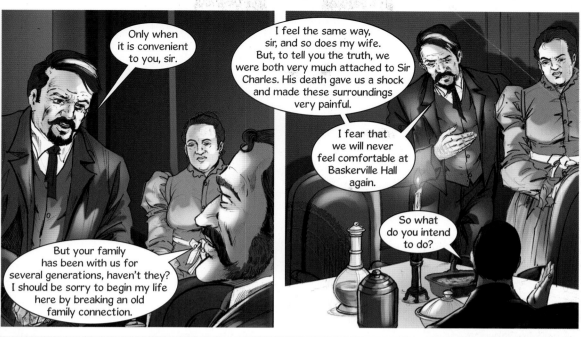

Only when it is convenient to you, sir.

I feel the same way, sir, and so does my wife. But, to tell you the truth, we were both very much attached to Sir Charles. His death gave us a shock and made these surroundings very painful.

I fear that we will never feel comfortable at Baskerville Hall again.

So what do you intend to do?

But your family has been with us for several generations, haven't they? I should be sorry to begin my life here by breaking an old family connection.

I have no doubt, sir, that we will succeed in starting up some kind of business.

As you wish, Barrymore.

Sir, perhaps I should show you to your rooms.

HAWOOOOOO

It... it must be the wind?

Dear Holmes, there is a great deal of superstition surrounding the Baskerville Hound. In fact, this evening, I heard a terrible noise, like a wolf's cry, somewhere in the moor.

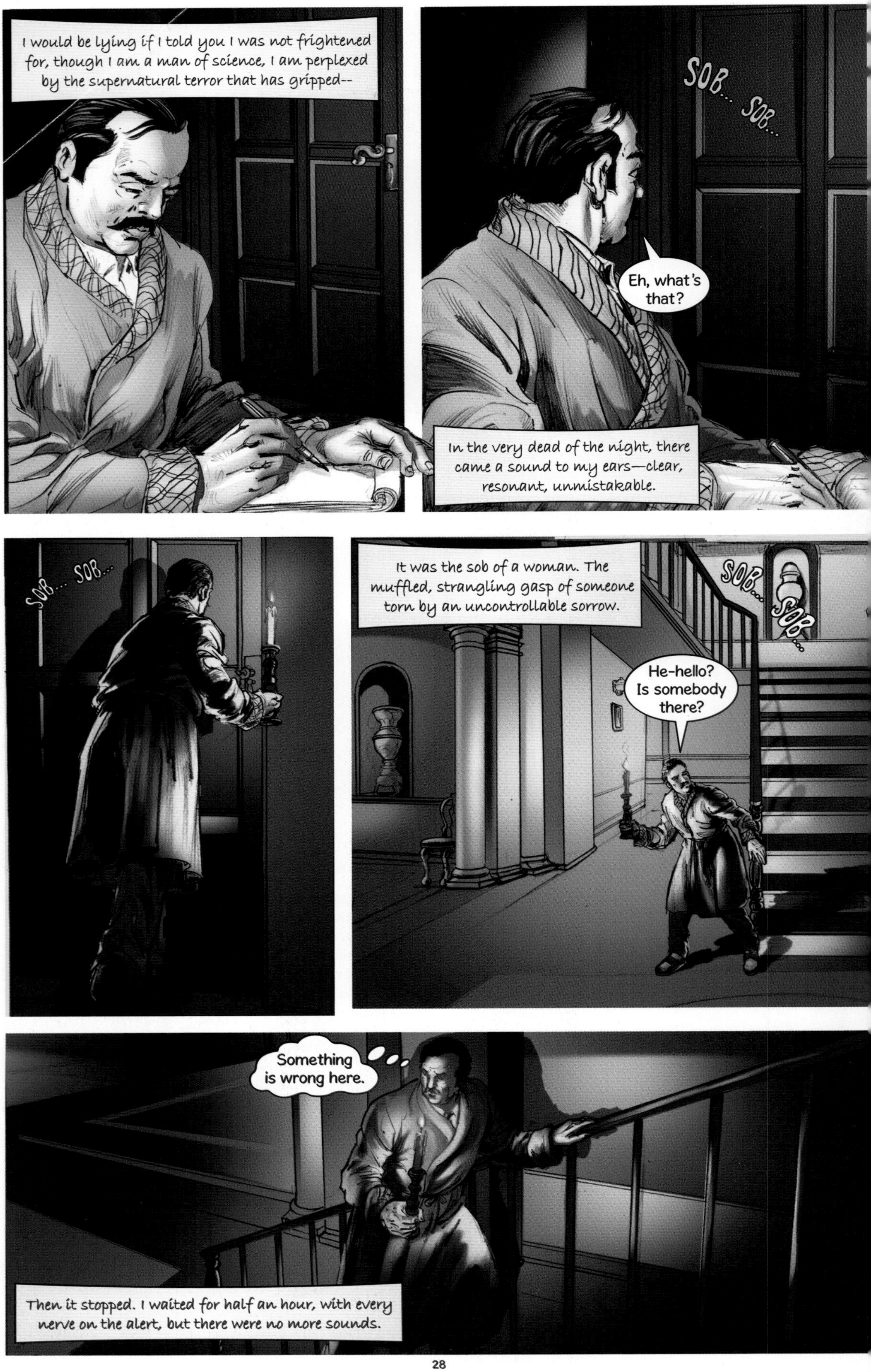
I would be lying if I told you I was not frightened for, though I am a man of science, I am perplexed by the supernatural terror that has gripped--
SOB... SOB...
Eh, what's that?
In the very dead of the night, there came a sound to my ears—clear, resonant, unmistakable.
SOB... SOB...
It was the sob of a woman. The muffled, strangling gasp of someone torn by an uncontrollable sorrow.
SOB... SOB...
He-hello? Is somebody there?
Something is wrong here.
Then it stopped. I waited for half an hour, with every nerve on the alert, but there were no more sounds.

The next morning...

Did you hear a woman crying during the night?

That is strange because, when I was half asleep, I thought I heard something of the sort. I waited for some time, but it didn't continue, so I decided that I had been dreaming.

I heard it distinctly, and I am sure that it was the sob of a woman.

We must ask about this right away.

Sir Henry rang the bell and asked Barrymore whether he could account for our experience.

There are only two women in the house, Sir Henry. One is the scullery-maid, who sleeps in the other wing. The other is my wife, and I can confirm that the sound did not come from her.

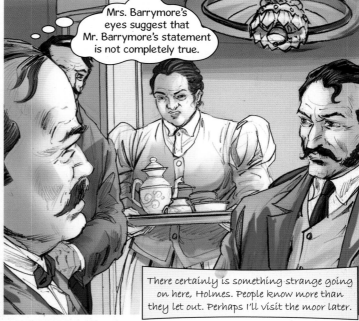

Mrs. Barrymore's eyes suggest that Mr. Barrymore's statement is not completely true.

There certainly is something strange going on here, Holmes. People know more than they let out. Perhaps I'll visit the moor later.

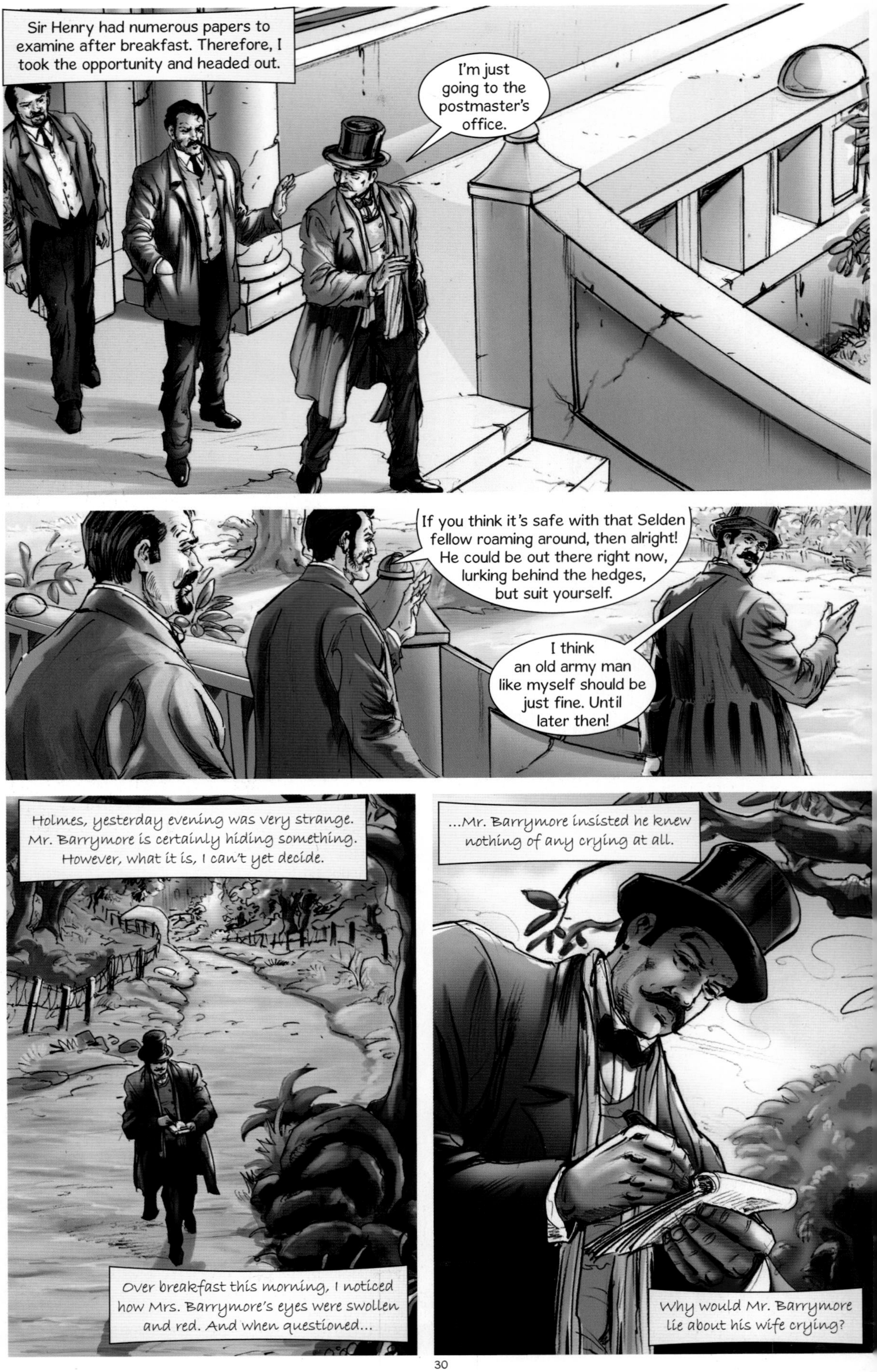
Sir Henry had numerous papers to examine after breakfast. Therefore, I took the opportunity and headed out.
I'm just going to the postmaster's office.
If you think it's safe with that Selden fellow roaming around, then alright! He could be out there right now, lurking behind the hedges, but suit yourself.
I think an old army man like myself should be just fine. Until later then!
Holmes, yesterday evening was very strange. Mr. Barrymore is certainly hiding something. However, what it is, I can't yet decide.
Over breakfast this morning, I noticed how Mrs. Barrymore's eyes were swollen and red. And when questioned...
...Mr. Barrymore insisted he knew nothing of any crying at all.
Why would Mr. Barrymore lie about his wife crying?

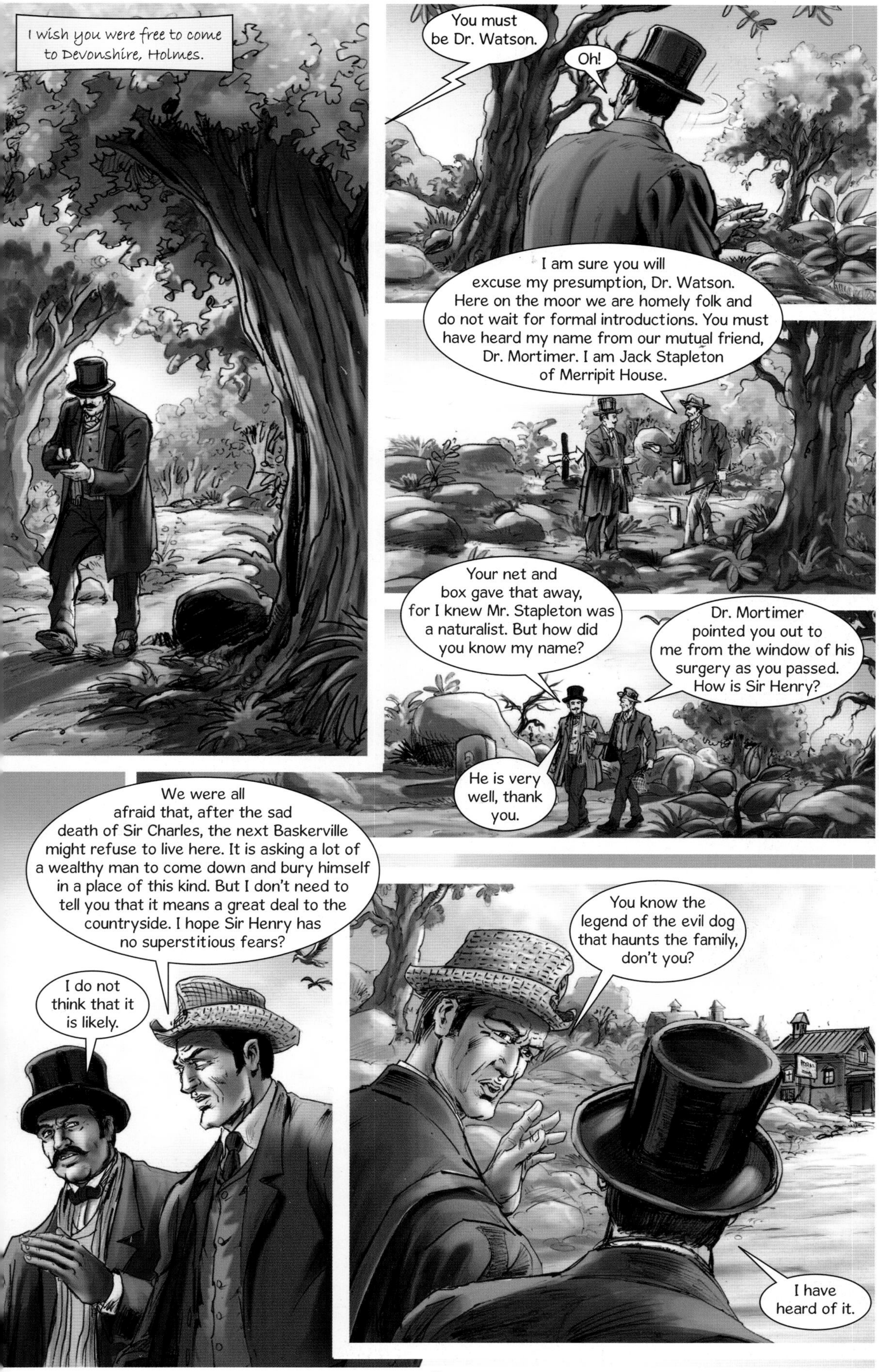
I wish you were free to come to Devonshire, Holmes.
You must be Dr. Watson.
Oh!
I am sure you will excuse my presumption, Dr. Watson. Here on the moor we are homely folk and do not wait for formal introductions. You must have heard my name from our mutual friend, Dr. Mortimer. I am Jack Stapleton of Merripit House.
Your net and box gave that away, for I knew Mr. Stapleton was a naturalist. But how did you know my name?
Dr. Mortimer pointed you out to me from the window of his surgery as you passed. How is Sir Henry?
He is very well, thank you.
We were all afraid that, after the sad death of Sir Charles, the next Baskerville might refuse to live here. It is asking a lot of a wealthy man to come down and bury himself in a place of this kind. But I don't need to tell you that it means a great deal to the countryside. I hope Sir Henry has no superstitious fears?
I do not think that it is likely.
You know the legend of the evil dog that haunts the family, don't you?
I have heard of it.

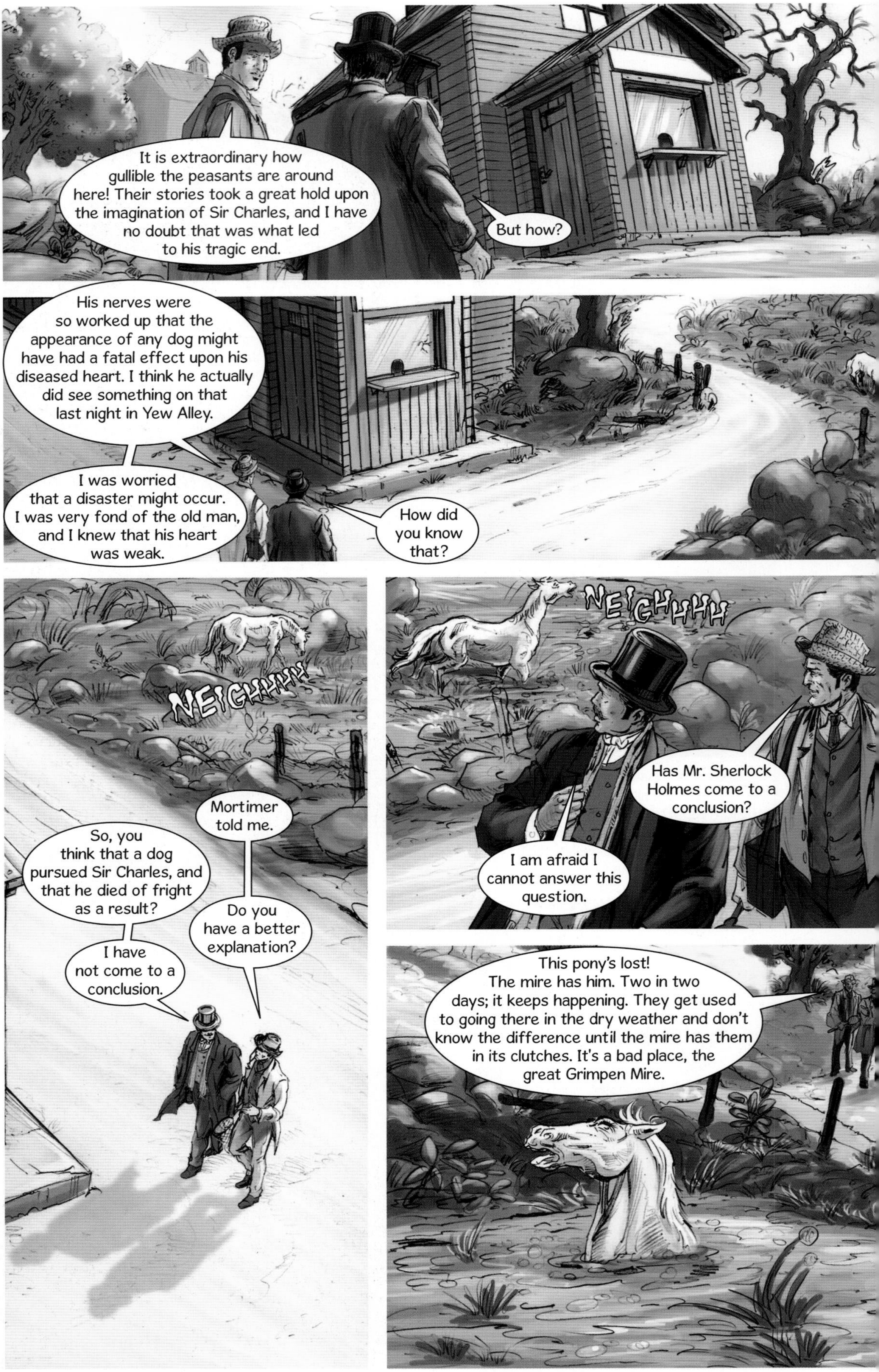
It is extraordinary how gullible the peasants are around here! Their stories took a great hold upon the imagination of Sir Charles, and I have no doubt that was what led to his tragic end.
But how?
His nerves were so worked up that the appearance of any dog might have had a fatal effect upon his diseased heart. I think he actually did see something on that last night in Yew Alley.
I was worried that a disaster might occur. I was very fond of the old man, and I knew that his heart was weak.
How did you know that?
NEIGHHHH
Mortimer told me.
So, you think that a dog pursued Sir Charles, and that he died of fright as a result?
Do you have a better explanation?
I have not come to a conclusion.
NEIGHHHH
Has Mr. Sherlock Holmes come to a conclusion?
I am afraid I cannot answer this question.
This pony's lost! The mire has him. Two in two days; it keeps happening. They get used to going there in the dry weather and don't know the difference until the mire has them in its clutches. It's a bad place, the great Grimpen Mire.

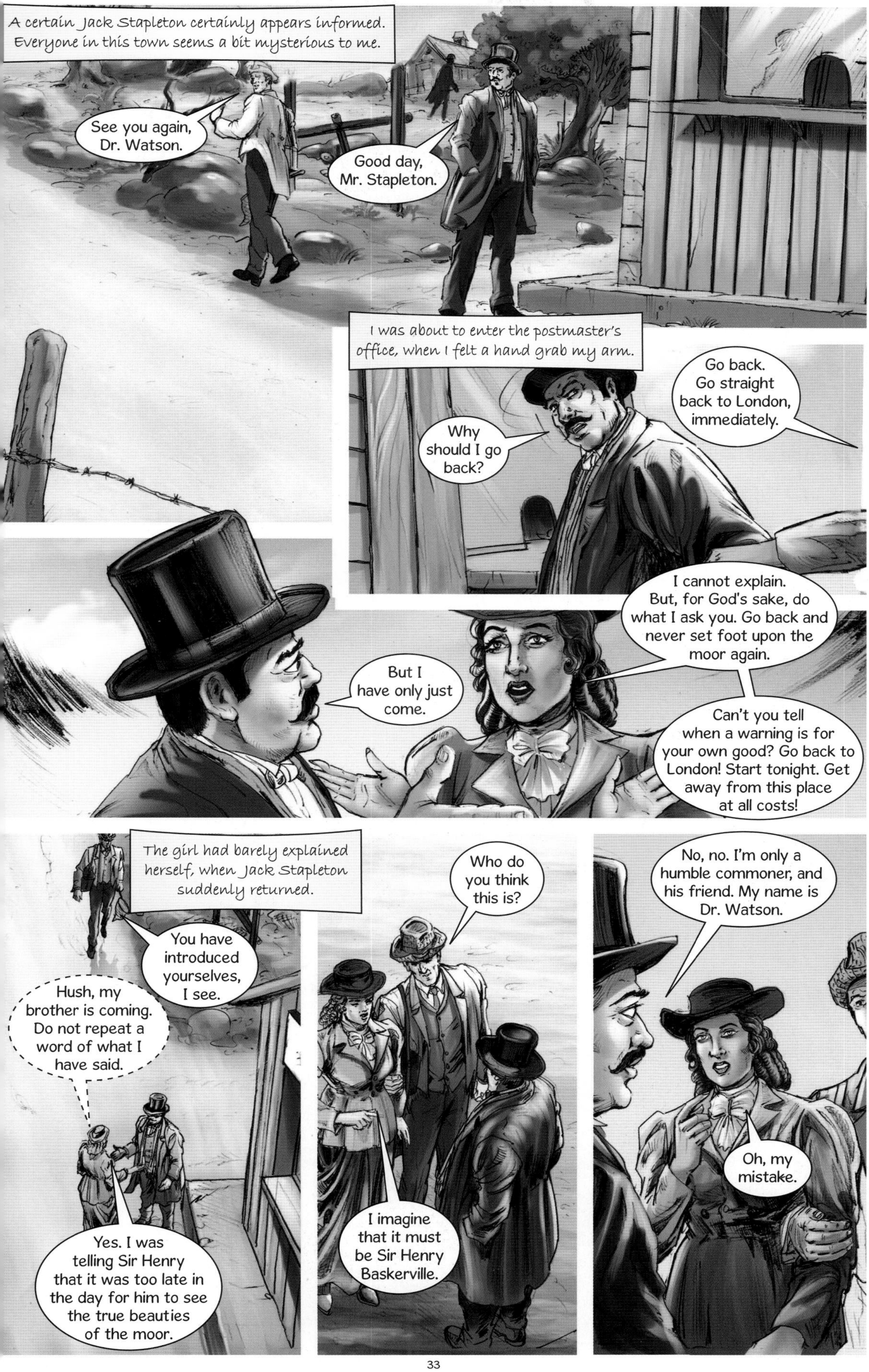
A certain Jack Stapleton certainly appears informed. Everyone in this town seems a bit mysterious to me.
See you again, Dr. Watson.
Good day, Mr. Stapleton.
I was about to enter the postmaster's office, when I felt a hand grab my arm.
Go back. Go straight back to London, immediately.
Why should I go back?
I cannot explain. But, for God's sake, do what I ask you. Go back and never set foot upon the moor again.
But I have only just come.
Can't you tell when a warning is for your own good? Go back to London! Start tonight. Get away from this place at all costs!
The girl had barely explained herself, when Jack Stapleton suddenly returned.
You have introduced yourselves, I see.
Hush, my brother is coming. Do not repeat a word of what I have said.
Yes. I was telling Sir Henry that it was too late in the day for him to see the true beauties of the moor.
Who do you think this is?
I imagine that it must be Sir Henry Baskerville.
No, no. I'm only a humble commoner, and his friend. My name is Dr. Watson.
Oh, my mistake.

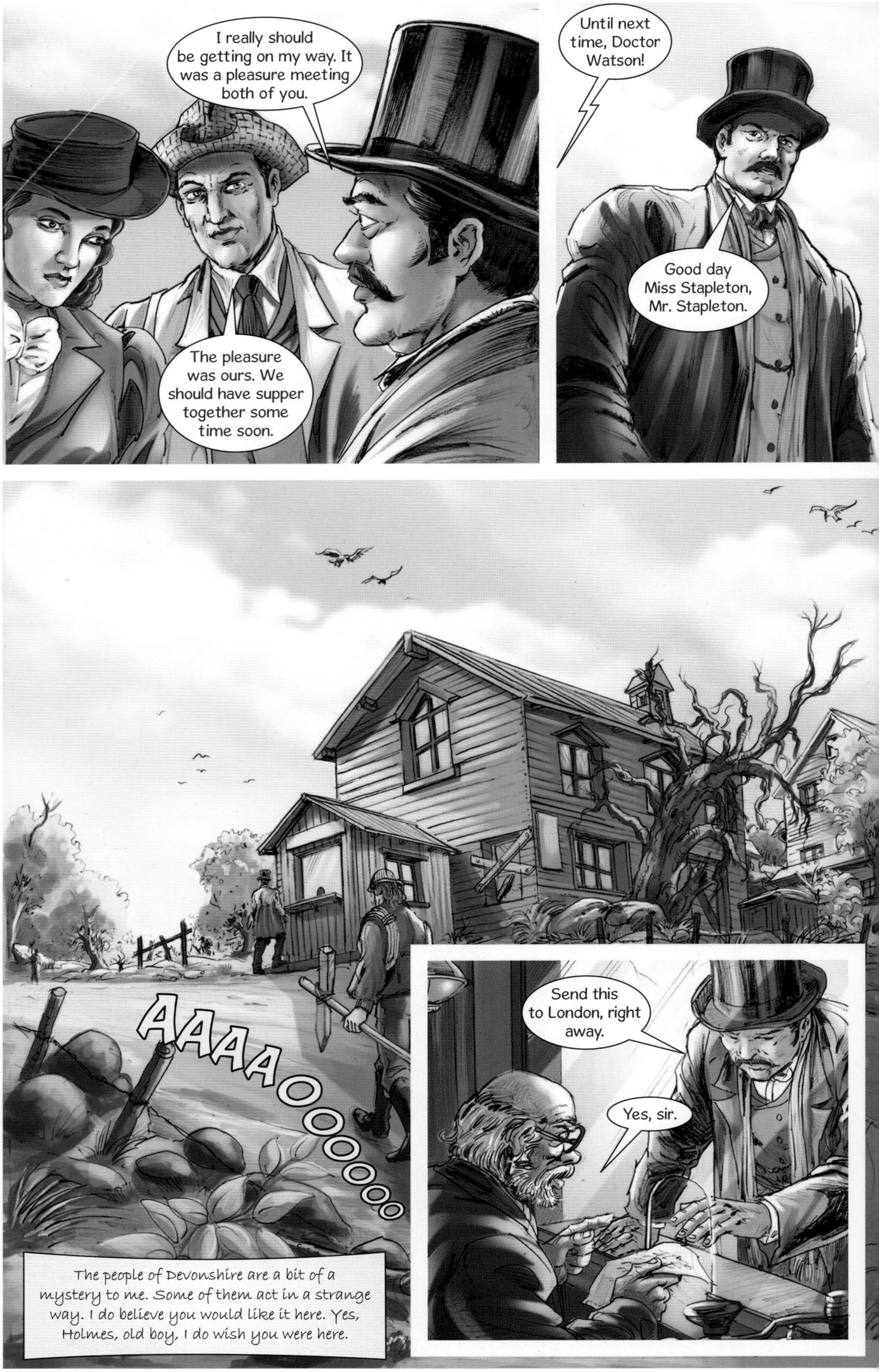

I really should be getting on my way. It was a pleasure meeting both of you.
The pleasure was ours. We should have supper together some time soon.
Until next time, Doctor Watson!
Good day Miss Stapleton, Mr. Stapleton.
AAAAAOOOOOOO
Send this to London, right away.
Yes, sir.
The people of Devonshire are a bit of a mystery to me. Some of them act in a strange way. I do believe you would like it here. Yes, Holmes, old boy, I do wish you were here.

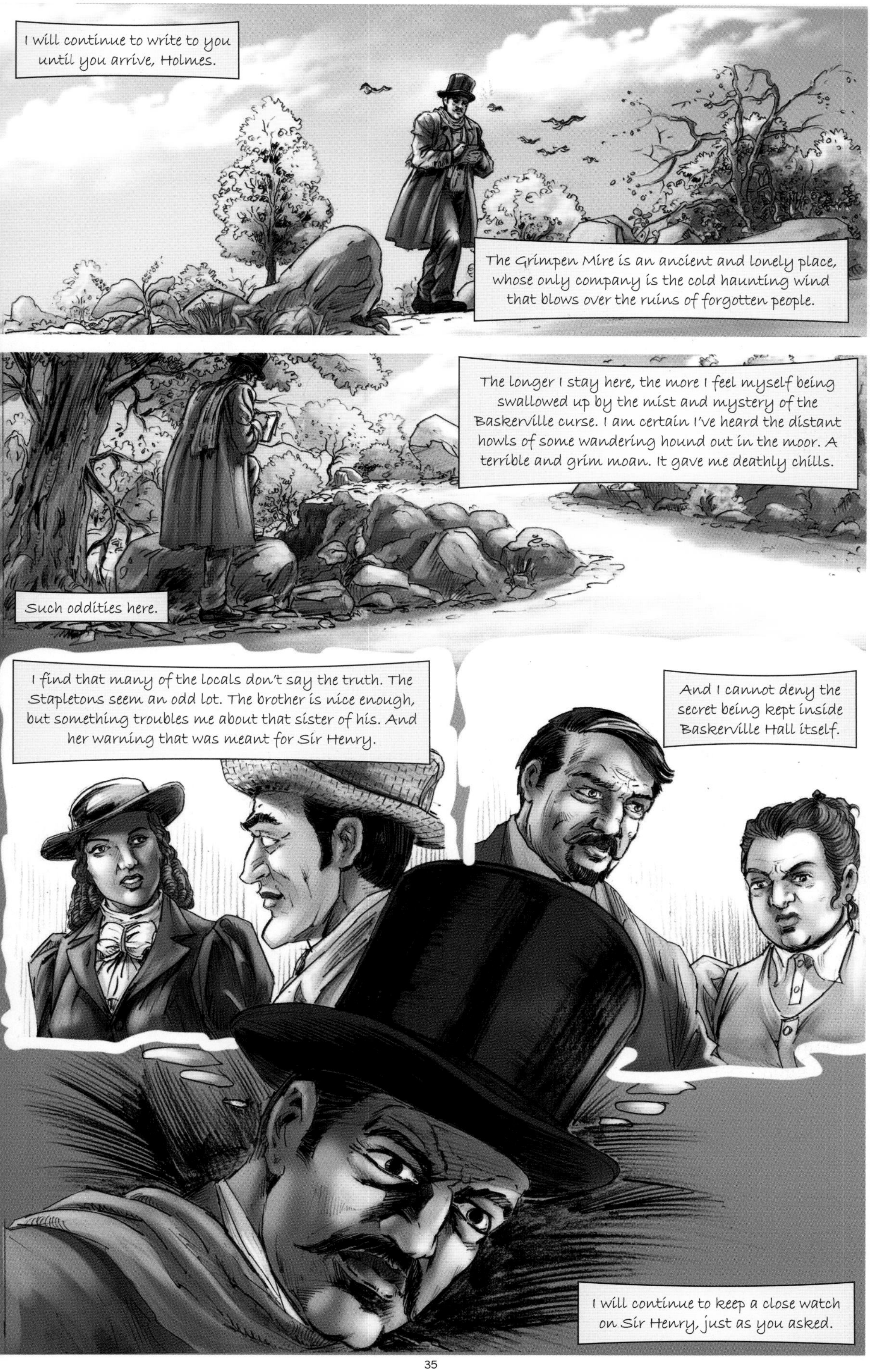

I will continue to write to you until you arrive, Holmes.
The Grimpen Mire is an ancient and lonely place, whose only company is the cold haunting wind that blows over the ruins of forgotten people.
The longer I stay here, the more I feel myself being swallowed up by the mist and mystery of the Baskerville curse. I am certain I've heard the distant howls of some wandering hound out in the moor. A terrible and grim moan. It gave me deathly chills.
Such oddities here.
I find that many of the locals don't say the truth. The Stapletons seem an odd lot. The brother is nice enough, but something troubles me about that sister of his. And her warning that was meant for Sir Henry.
And I cannot deny the secret being kept inside Baskerville Hall itself.
I will continue to keep a close watch on Sir Henry, just as you asked.

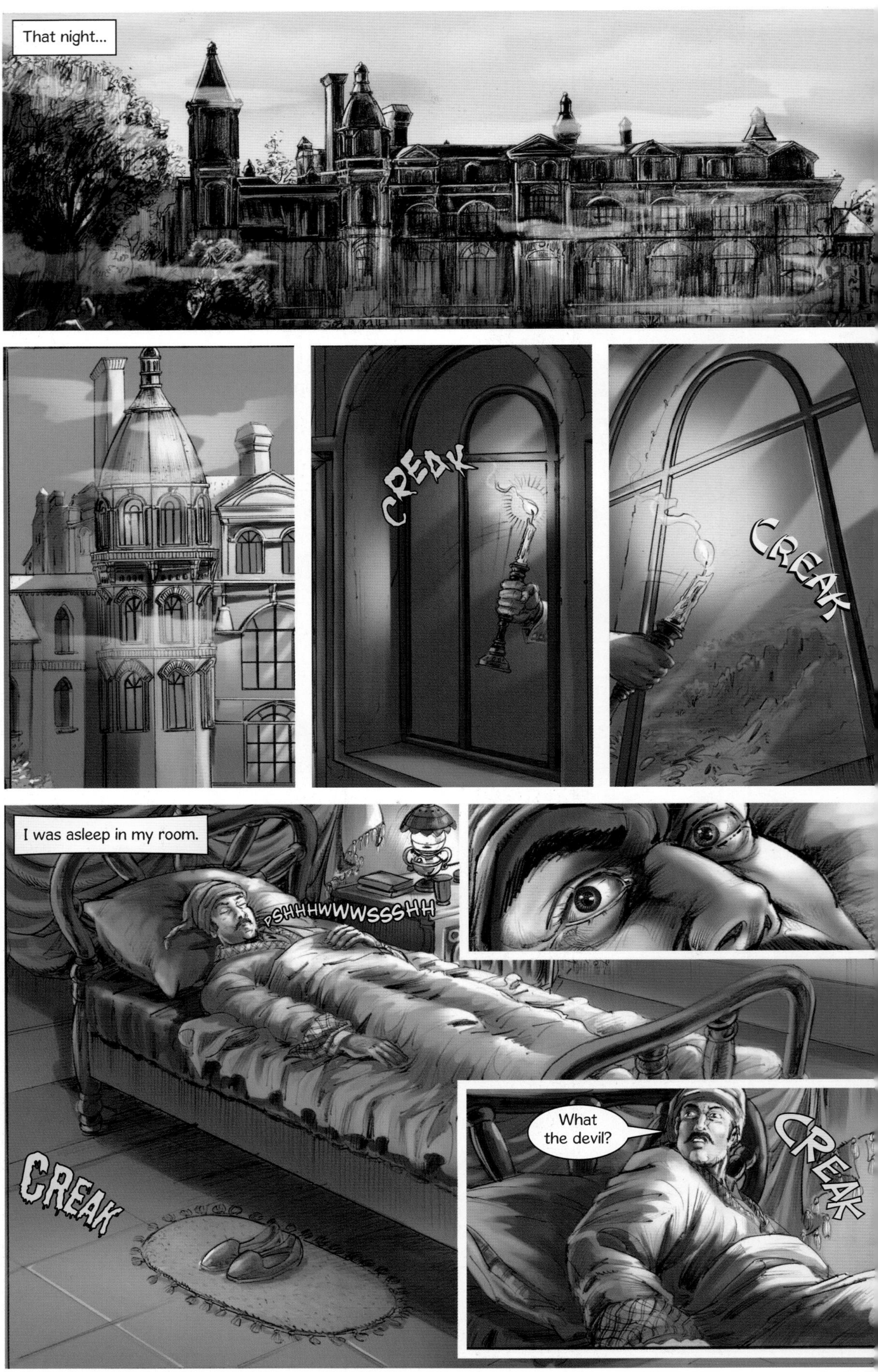
That night...
CREAK
CREAK
I was asleep in my room.
PSHHHWWWSSSHH
CREAK
What the devil?
CREAK

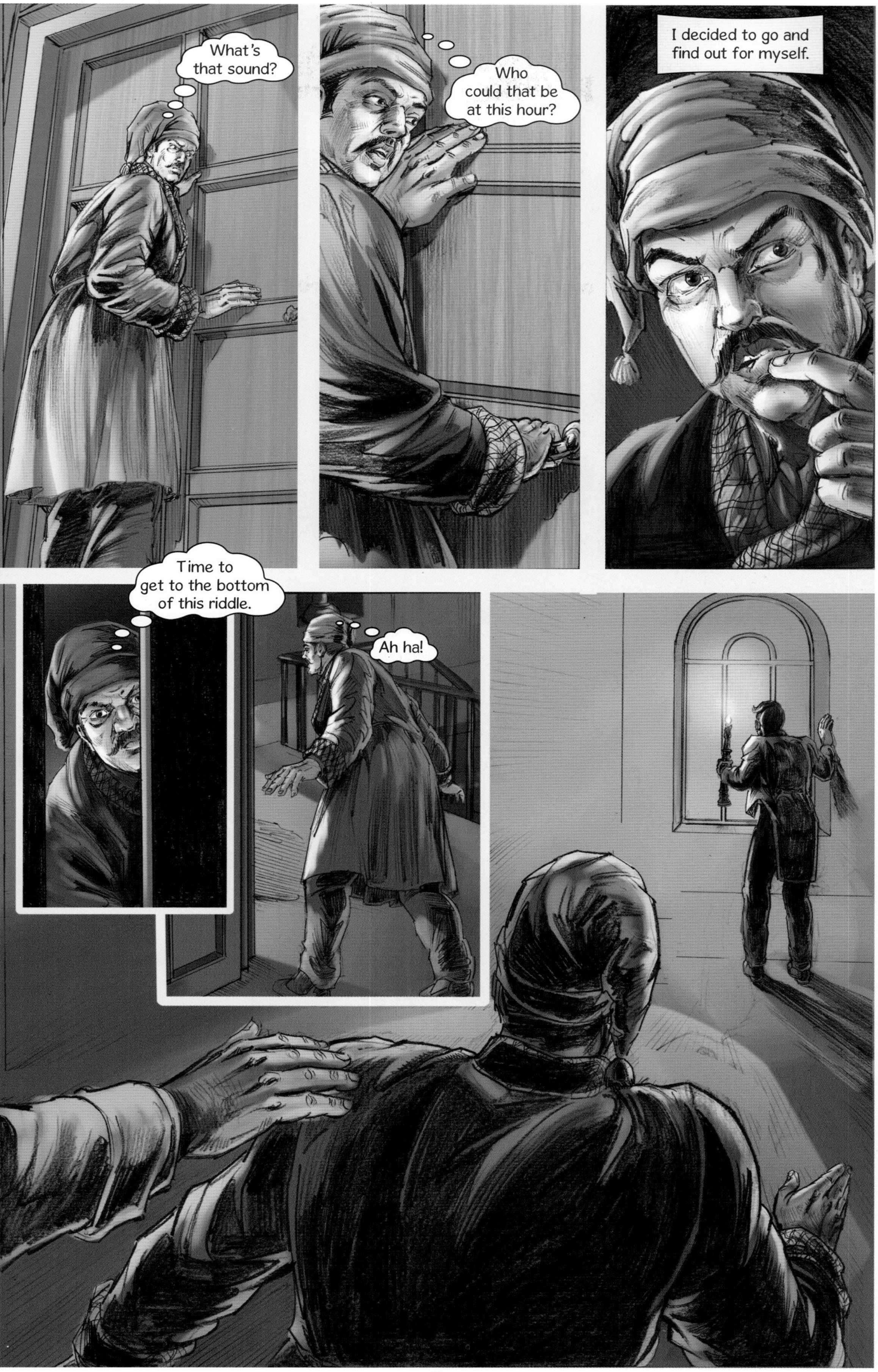
What's that sound?
Who could that be at this hour?
I decided to go and find out for myself.
Time to get to the bottom of this riddle.
Ah ha!

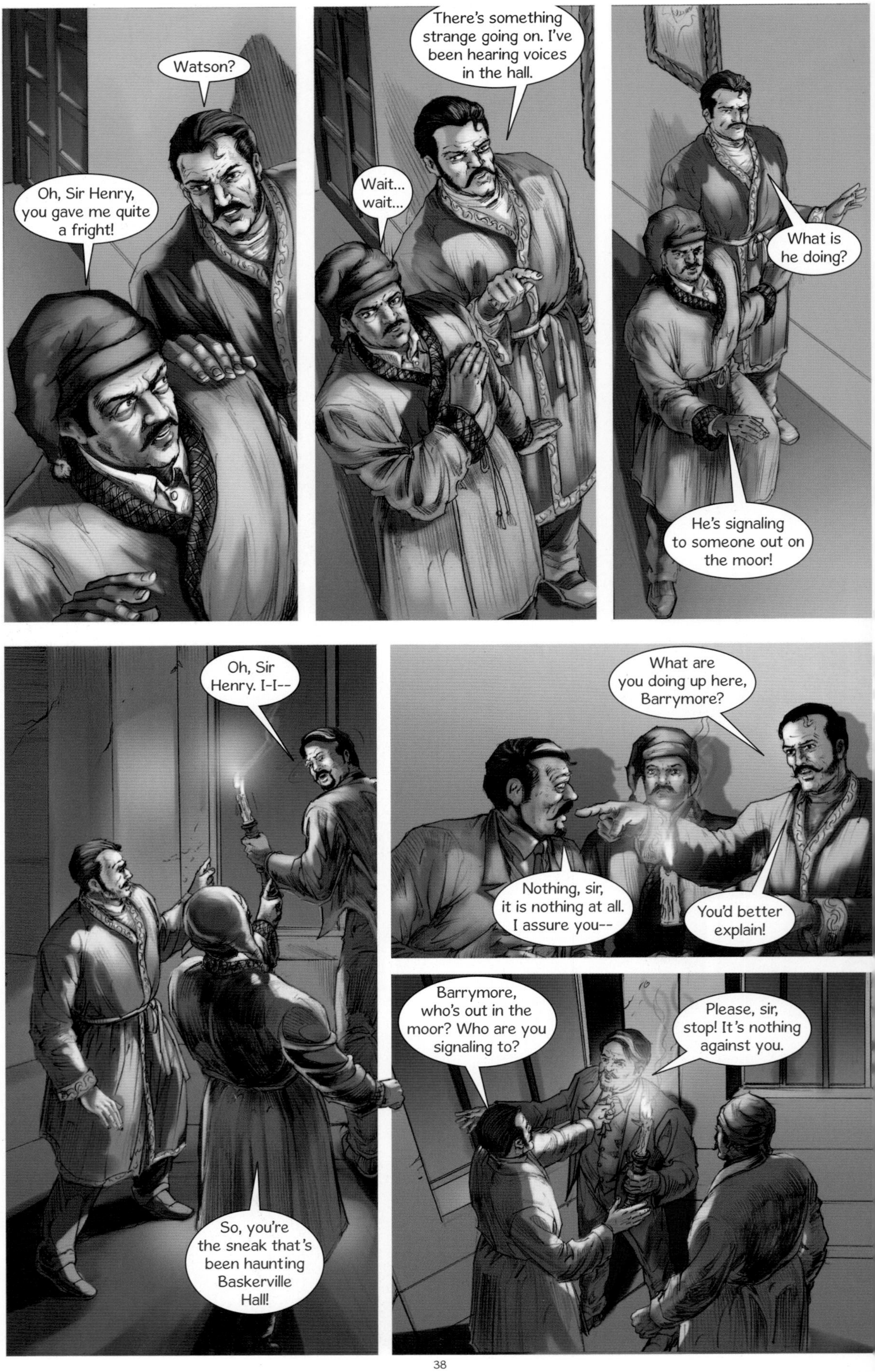
Watson?
Oh, Sir Henry, you gave me quite a fright!
There's something strange going on. I've been hearing voices in the hall.
Wait... wait...
What is he doing?
He's signaling to someone out on the moor!
Oh, Sir Henry. I-I--
So, you're the sneak that's been haunting Baskerville Hall!
What are you doing up here, Barrymore?
Nothing, sir, it is nothing at all. I assure you--
You'd better explain!
Barrymore, who's out in the moor? Who are you signaling to?
Please, sir, stop! It's nothing against you.

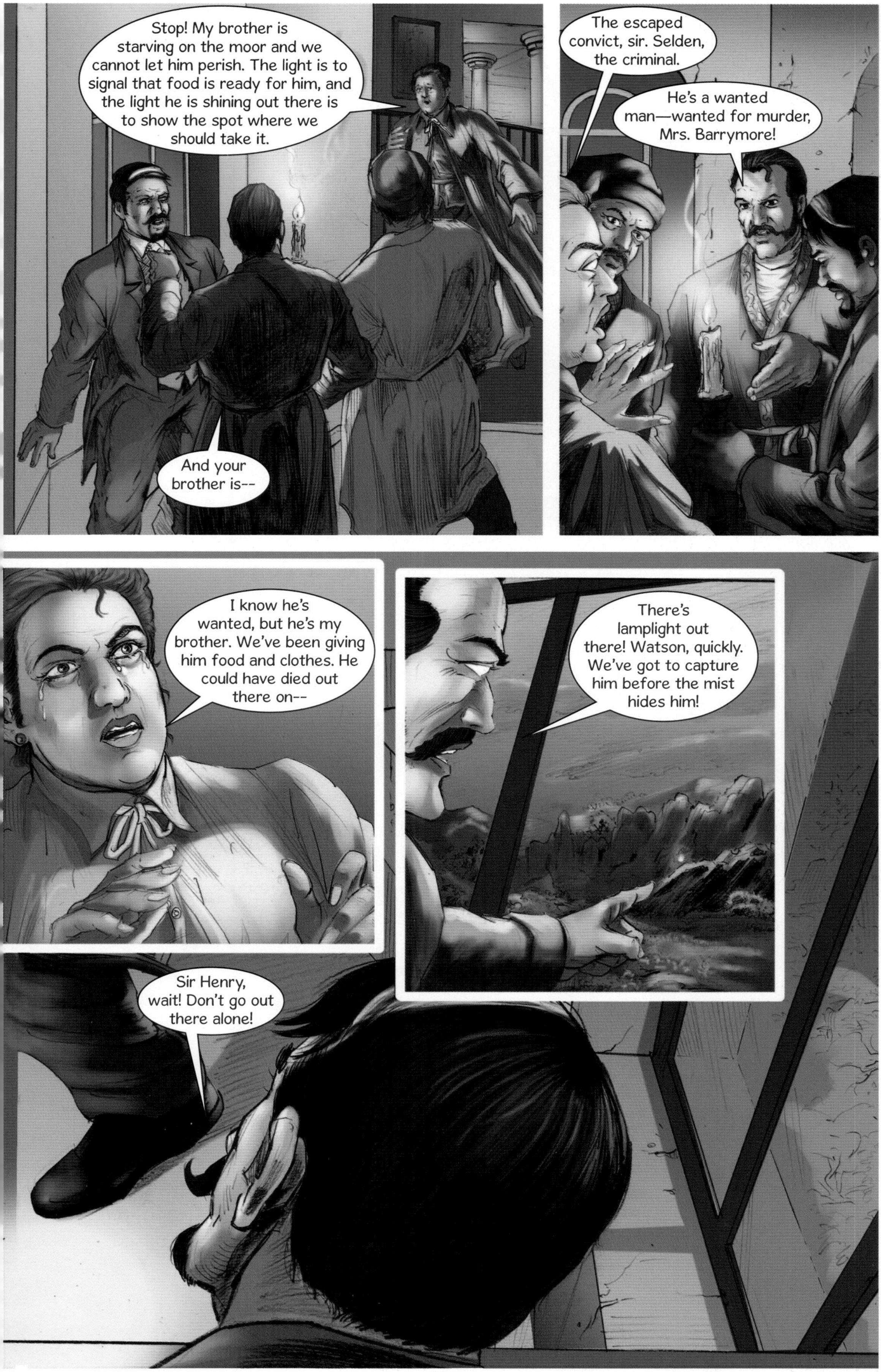
Stop! My brother is starving on the moor and we cannot let him perish. The light is to signal that food is ready for him, and the light he is shining out there is to show the spot where we should take it.
And your brother is--
The escaped convict, sir. Selden, the criminal.
He's a wanted man—wanted for murder, Mrs. Barrymore!
I know he's wanted, but he's my brother. We've been giving him food and clothes. He could have died out there on--
There's lamplight out there! Watson, quickly. We've got to capture him before the mist hides him!
Sir Henry, wait! Don't go out there alone!

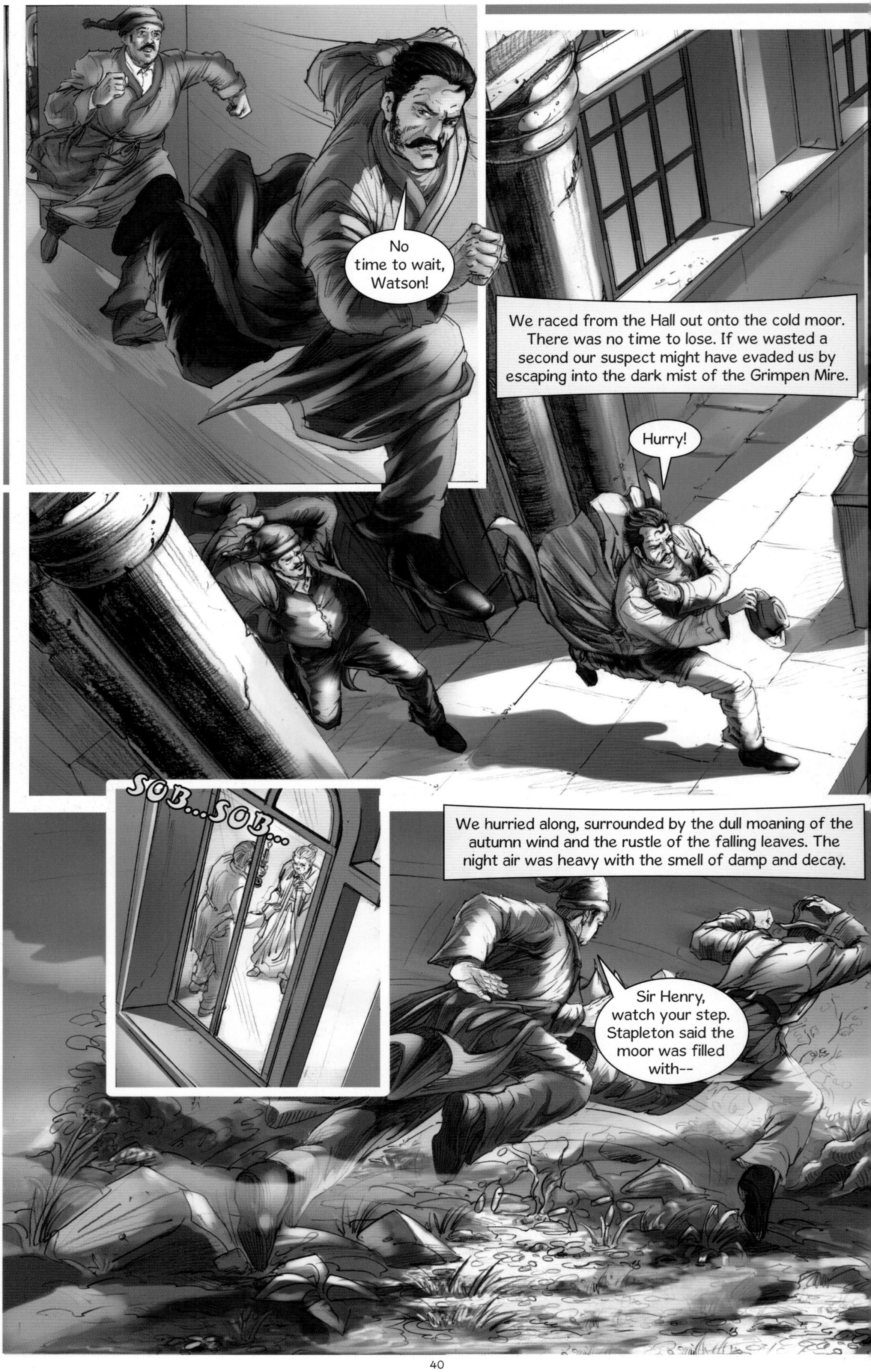
No time to wait, Watson!
We raced from the Hall out onto the cold moor. There was no time to lose. If we wasted a second our suspect might have evaded us by escaping into the dark mist of the Grimpen Mire.
Hurry!
SOB...SOB...
We hurried along, surrounded by the dull moaning of the autumn wind and the rustle of the falling leaves. The night air was heavy with the smell of damp and decay.
Sir Henry, watch your step. Stapleton said the moor was filled with--

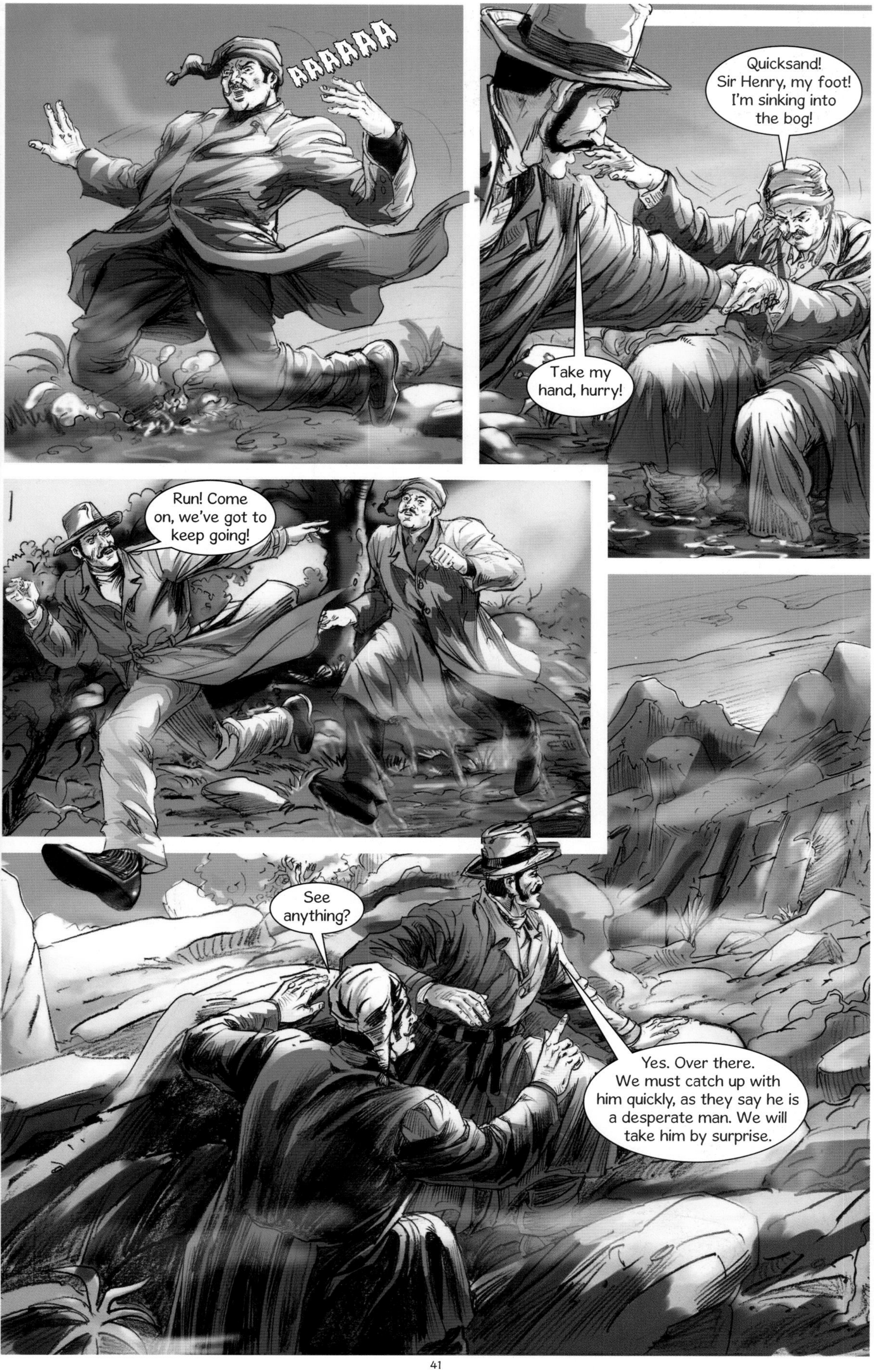
AAAAAA
Quicksand! Sir Henry, my foot! I'm sinking into the bog!
Take my hand, hurry!
Run! Come on, we've got to keep going!
See anything?
Yes. Over there. We must catch up with him quickly, as they say he is a desperate man. We will take him by surprise.

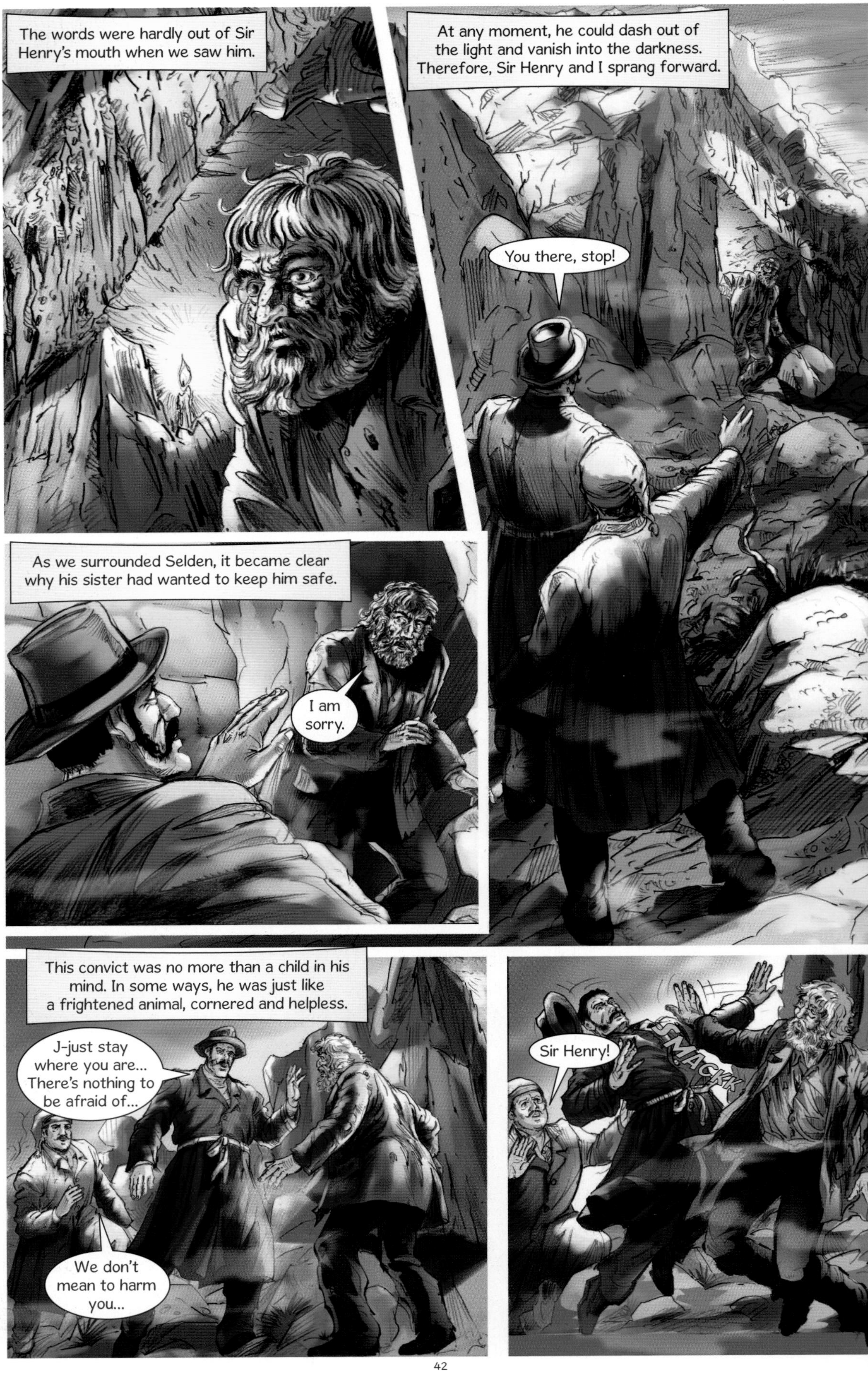
The words were hardly out of Sir Henry's mouth when we saw him.
At any moment, he could dash out of the light and vanish into the darkness. Therefore, Sir Henry and I sprang forward.
You there, stop!
As we surrounded Selden, it became clear why his sister had wanted to keep him safe.
I am sorry.
This convict was no more than a child in his mind. In some ways, he was just like a frightened animal, cornered and helpless.
J-just stay where you are... There's nothing to be afraid of...
We don't mean to harm you...
Sir Henry!
SMACKK

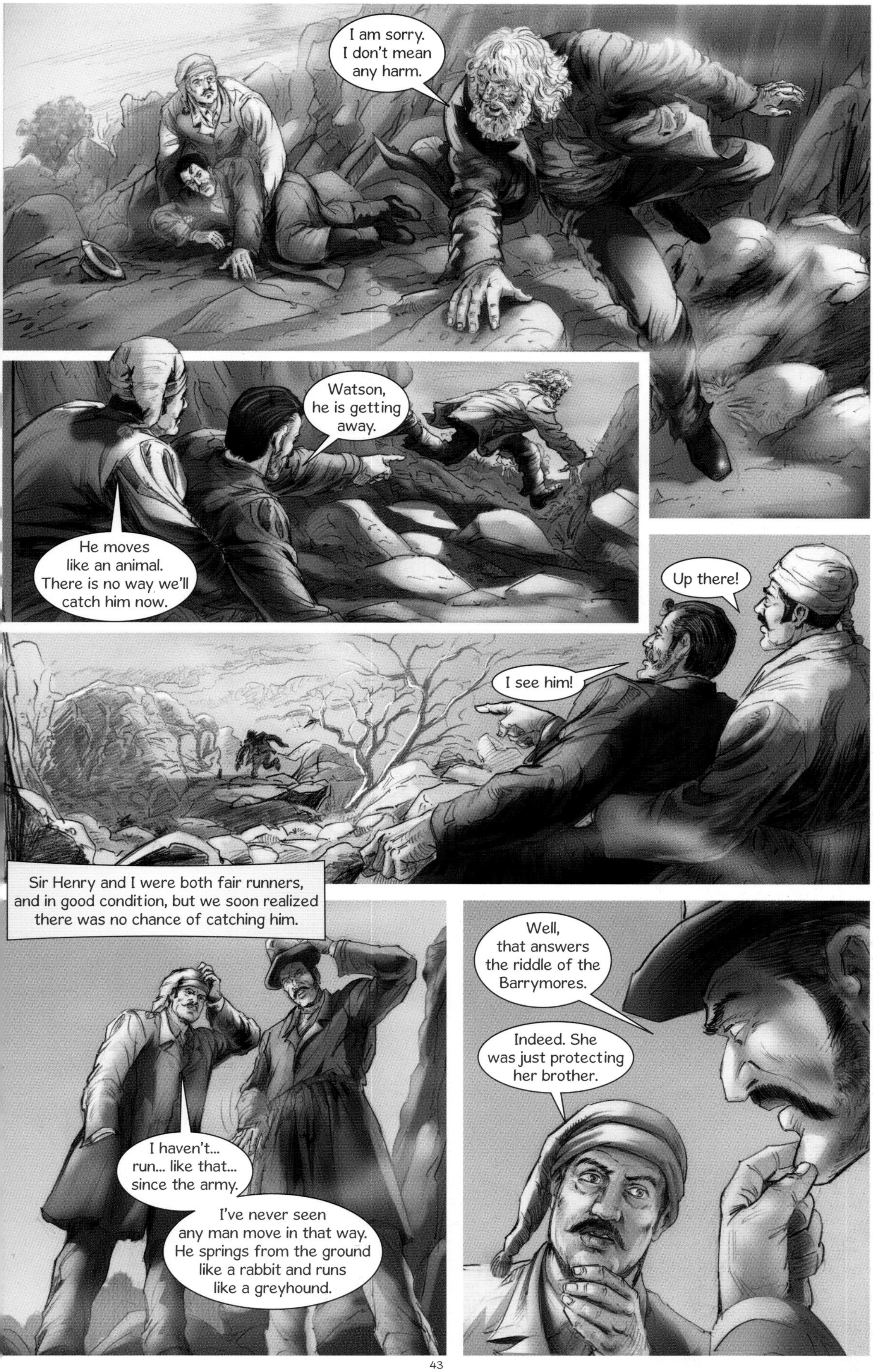

I am sorry. I don't mean any harm.
Watson, he is getting away.
He moves like an animal. There is no way we'll catch him now.
Up there!
I see him!
Sir Henry and I were both fair runners, and in good condition, but we soon realized there was no chance of catching him.
I haven't... run... like that... since the army.
I've never seen any man move in that way. He springs from the ground like a rabbit and runs like a greyhound.
Well, that answers the riddle of the Barrymores.
Indeed. She was just protecting her brother.

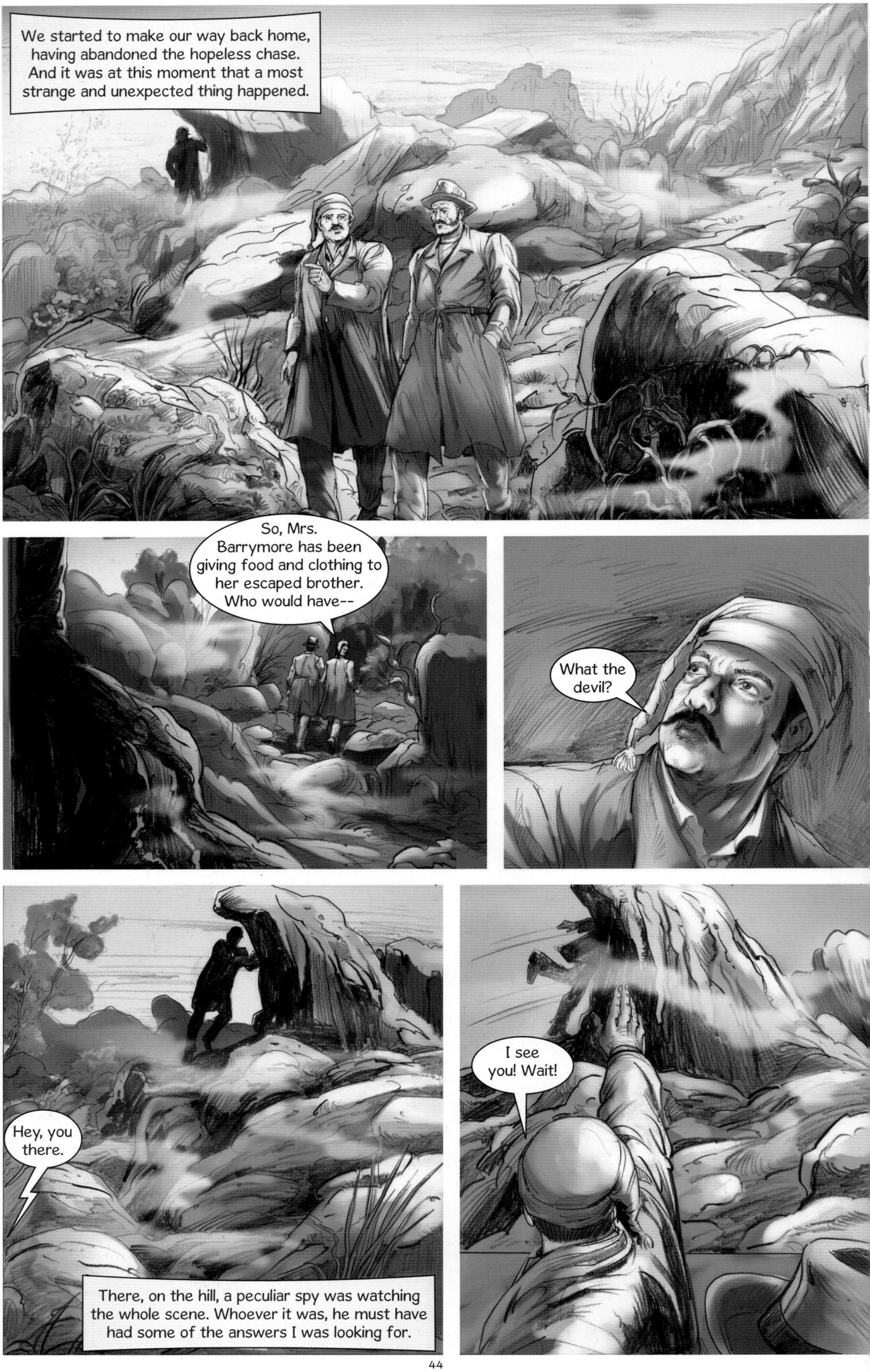
We started to make our way back home, having abandoned the hopeless chase. And it was at this moment that a most strange and unexpected thing happened.
So, Mrs. Barrymore has been giving food and clothing to her escaped brother. Who would have--
What the devil?
Hey, you there.
There, on the hill, a peculiar spy was watching the whole scene. Whoever it was, he must have had some of the answers I was looking for.
I see you! Wait!

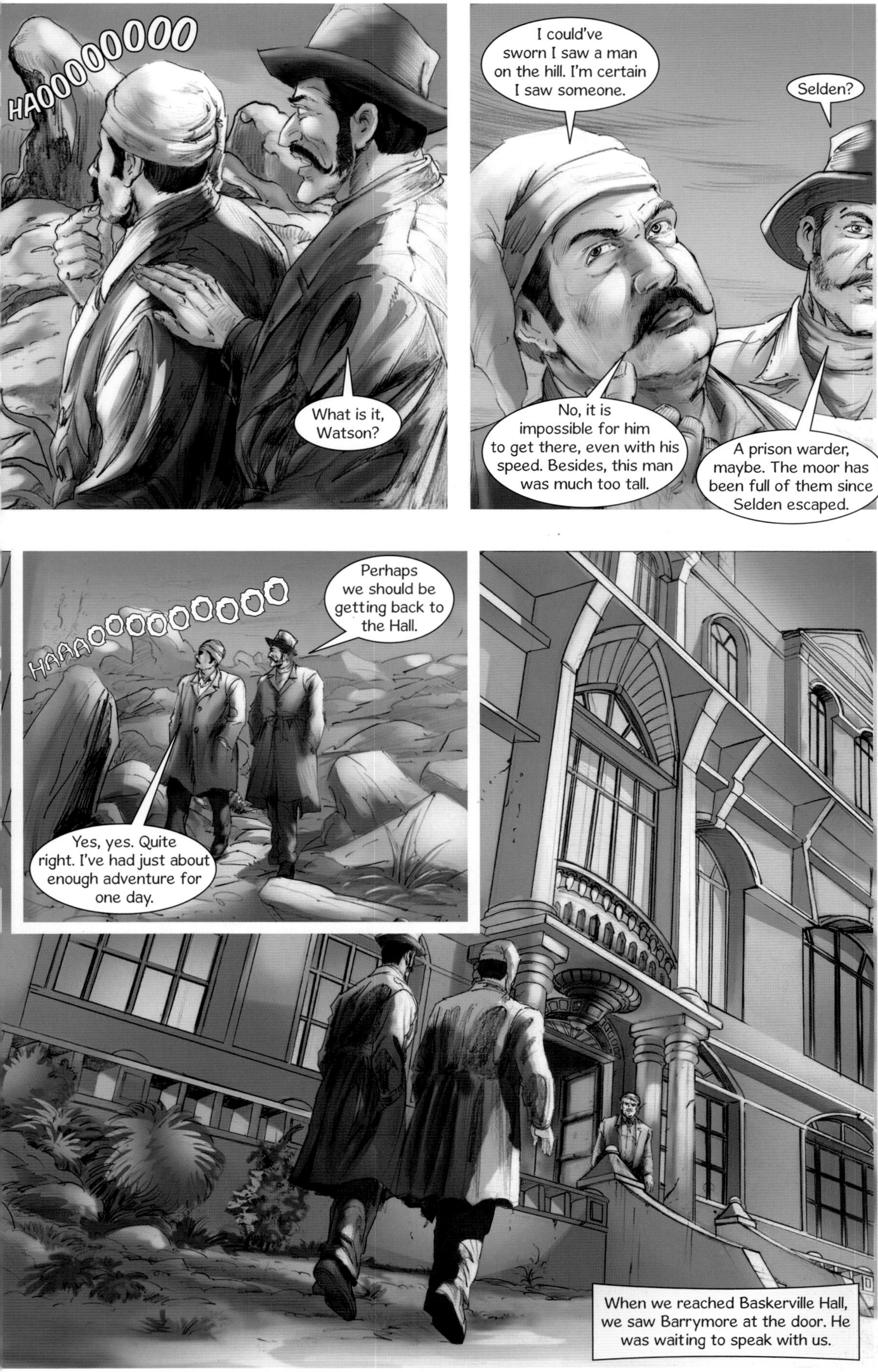
HAOOOOOOOO
What is it, Watson?
I could've sworn I saw a man on the hill. I'm certain I saw someone.
Selden?
No, it is impossible for him to get there, even with his speed. Besides, this man was much too tall.
A prison warder, maybe. The moor has been full of them since Selden escaped.
HAAAOOOOOOOOOOO
Perhaps we should be getting back to the Hall.
Yes, yes. Quite right. I've had just about enough adventure for one day.
When we reached Baskerville Hall, we saw Barrymore at the door. He was waiting to speak with us.

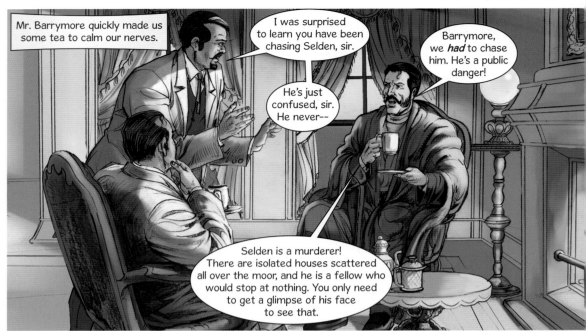

Mr. Barrymore quickly made us some tea to calm our nerves.

I was surprised to learn you have been chasing Selden, sir.

He's just confused, sir. He never--

Barrymore, we *had* to chase him. He's a public danger!

Selden is a murderer! There are isolated houses scattered all over the moor, and he is a fellow who would stop at nothing. You only need to get a glimpse of his face to see that.

He will never trouble anyone in this country again. I assure you, Sir Henry. In a few days, the necessary arrangements will have been made, and he will be on his way to South America.

Fine, Mr. Barrymore.

You've been so kind to us, sir, that I would like to do the best I can for you in return. I know something, about poor Sir Charles's death.

Do you know how he died?

I know why he was at the gate at that hour. It was to meet a woman.

To meet a woman! What's her name?

I don't know the name, sir, but I can give you the initials.

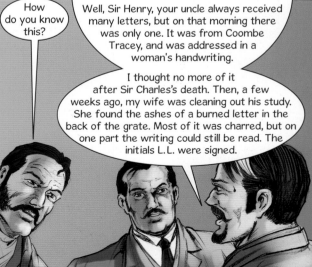

How do you know this?

Well, Sir Henry, your uncle always received many letters, but on that morning there was only one. It was from Coombe Tracey, and was addressed in a woman's handwriting.

I thought no more of it after Sir Charles's death. Then, a few weeks ago, my wife was cleaning out his study. She found the ashes of a burned letter in the back of the grate. Most of it was charred, but on one part the writing could still be read. The initials L.L. were signed.

46

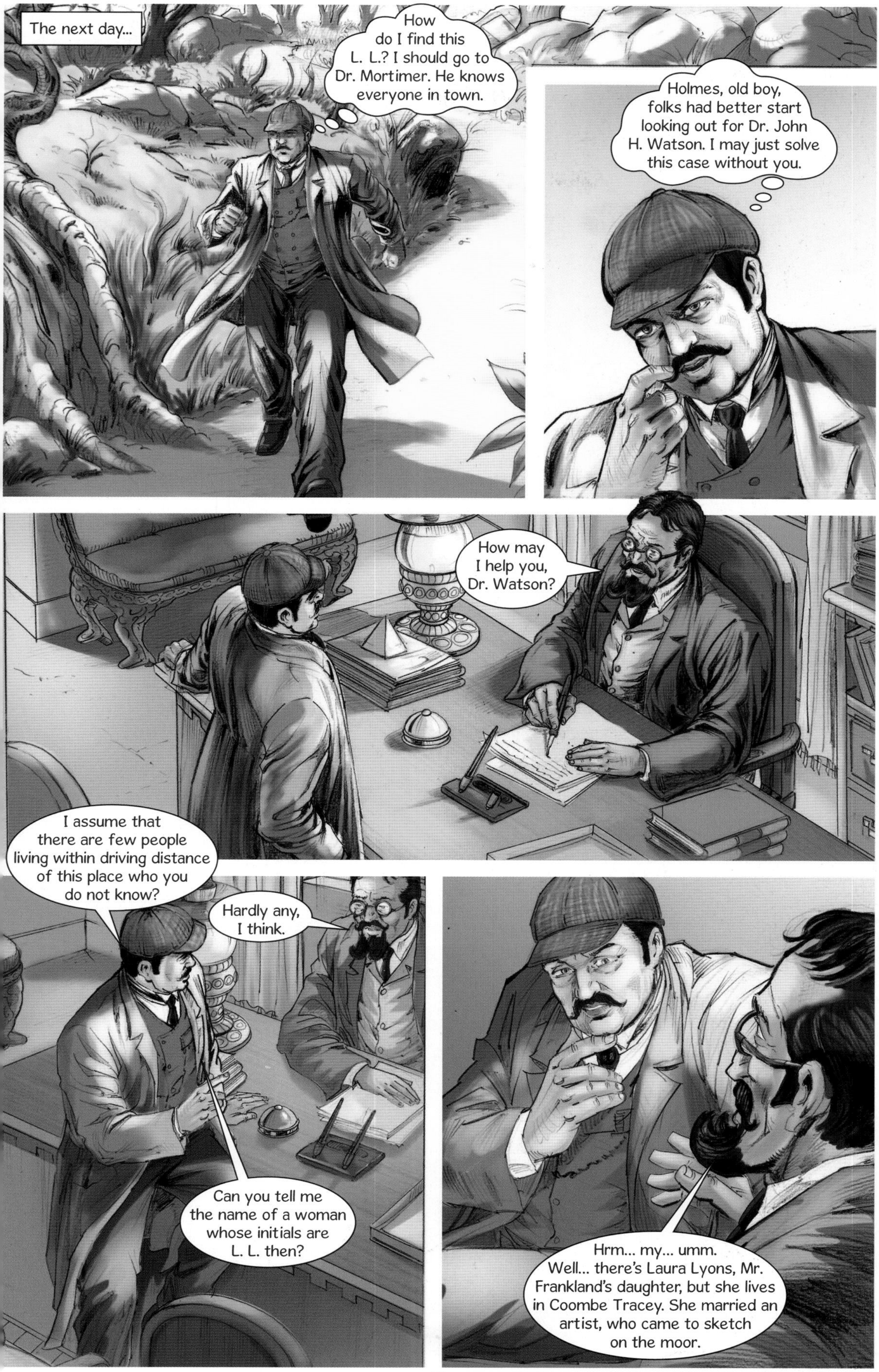
The next day...
How do I find this L. L.? I should go to Dr. Mortimer. He knows everyone in town.
Holmes, old boy, folks had better start looking out for Dr. John H. Watson. I may just solve this case without you.
How may I help you, Dr. Watson?
I assume that there are few people living within driving distance of this place who you do not know?
Hardly any, I think.
Can you tell me the name of a woman whose initials are L. L. then?
Hrm... my... umm. Well... there's Laura Lyons, Mr. Frankland's daughter, but she lives in Coombe Tracey. She married an artist, who came to sketch on the moor.

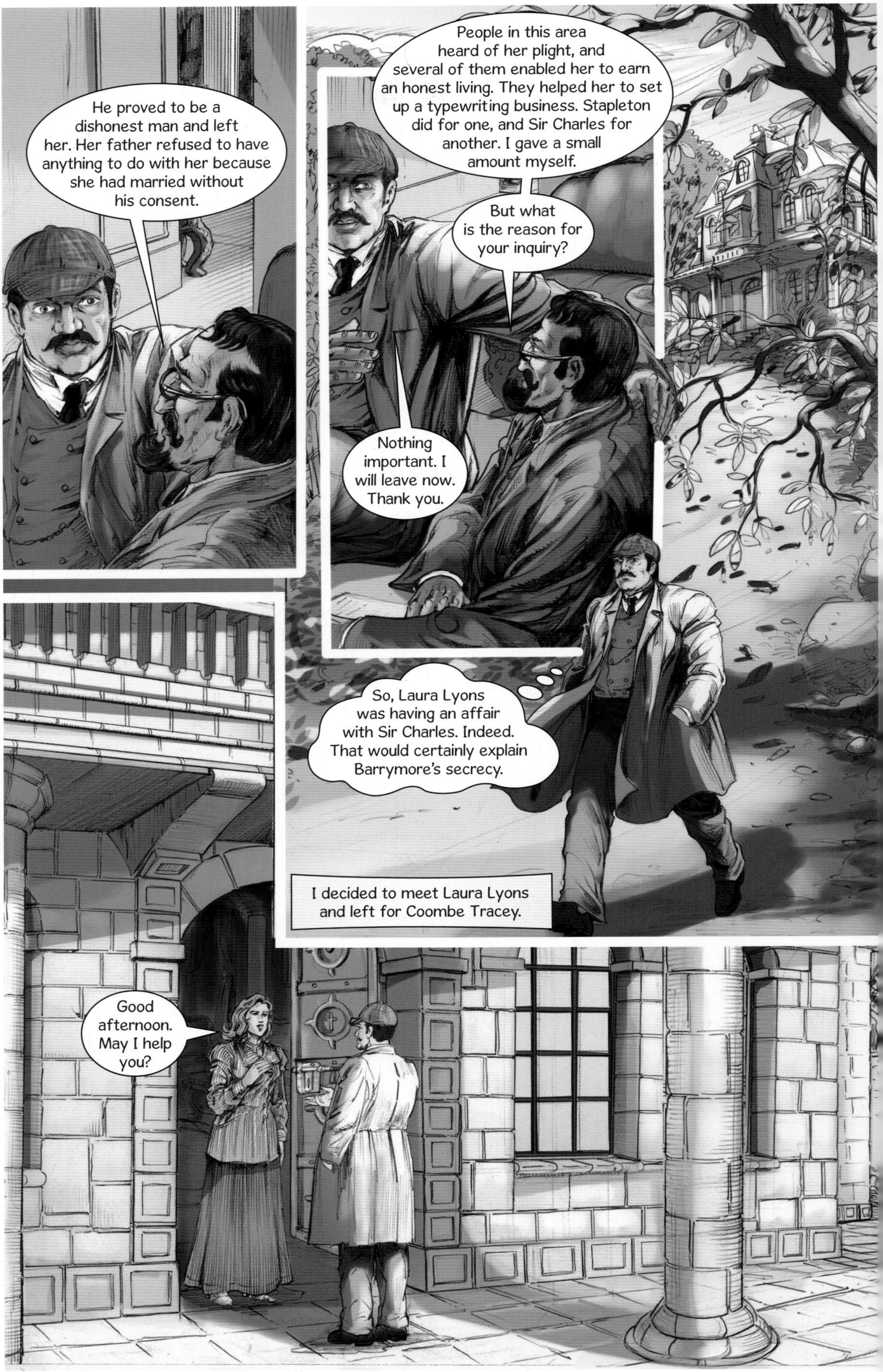
He proved to be a dishonest man and left her. Her father refused to have anything to do with her because she had married without his consent.
People in this area heard of her plight, and several of them enabled her to earn an honest living. They helped her to set up a typewriting business. Stapleton did for one, and Sir Charles for another. I gave a small amount myself.
But what is the reason for your inquiry?
Nothing important. I will leave now. Thank you.
So, Laura Lyons was having an affair with Sir Charles. Indeed. That would certainly explain Barrymore's secrecy.
I decided to meet Laura Lyons and left for Coombe Tracey.
Good afternoon. May I help you?

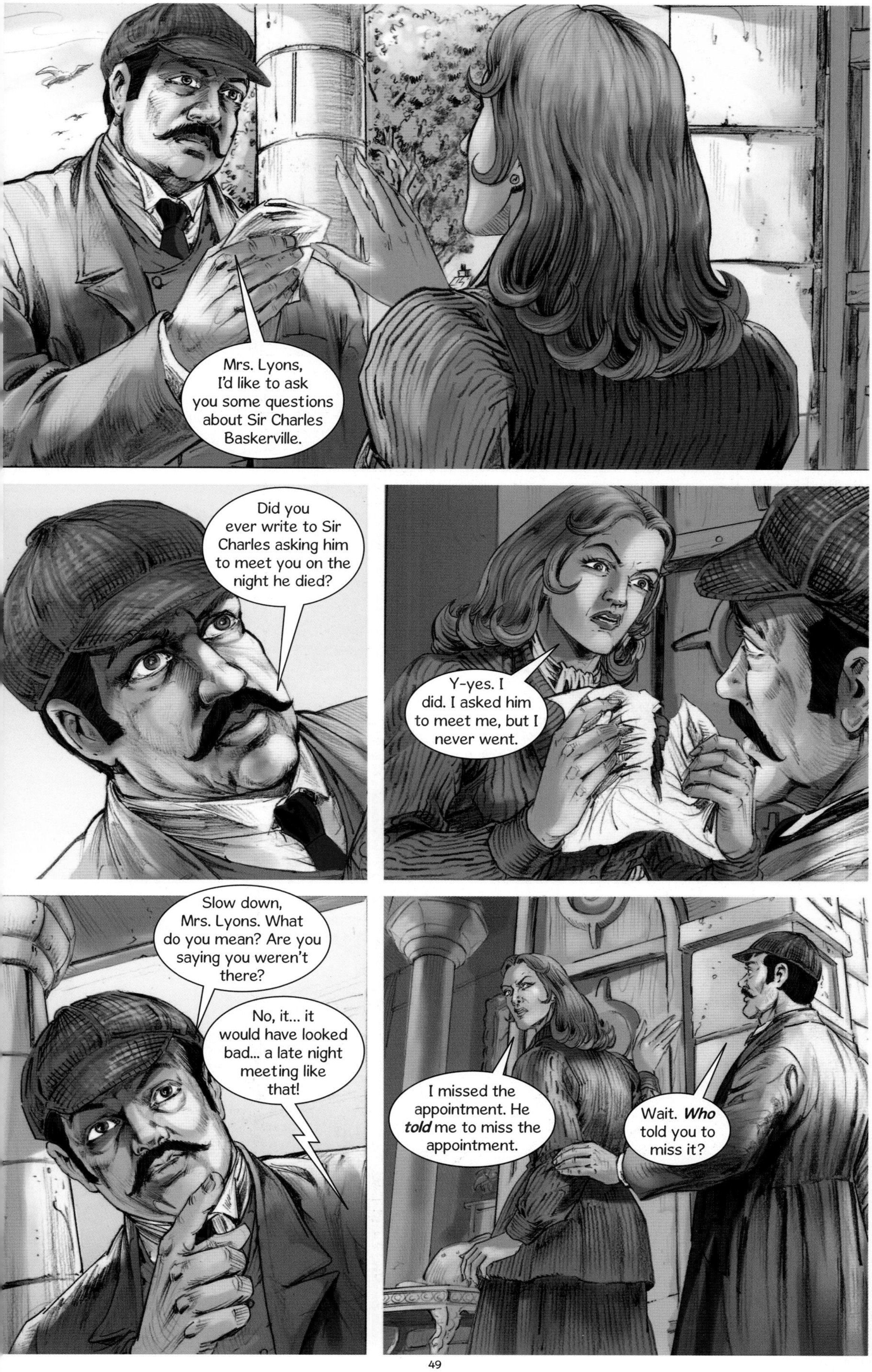
Mrs. Lyons, I'd like to ask you some questions about Sir Charles Baskerville.
Did you ever write to Sir Charles asking him to meet you on the night he died?
Y-yes. I did. I asked him to meet me, but I never went.
Slow down, Mrs. Lyons. What do you mean? Are you saying you weren't there?
No, it... it would have looked bad... a late night meeting like that!
I missed the appointment. He ***told*** me to miss the appointment.
Wait. ***Who*** told you to miss it?

Jack... Jack Stapleton.

Thank you, Mrs. Lyons.

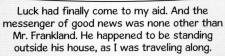

Luck had finally come to my aid. And the messenger of good news was none other than Mr. Frankland. He happened to be standing outside his house, as I was traveling along.

Good day, Dr. Watson. Give your horses some rest, and come in to have a glass of wine.

That would be great, Mr. Frankland. Thank you.

We talked at great length. Mr. Frankland was bragging about some thing or the other, when the conversation turned to the convict on the moor.

What do you know of him?

That a child takes food for him every day.

A child!

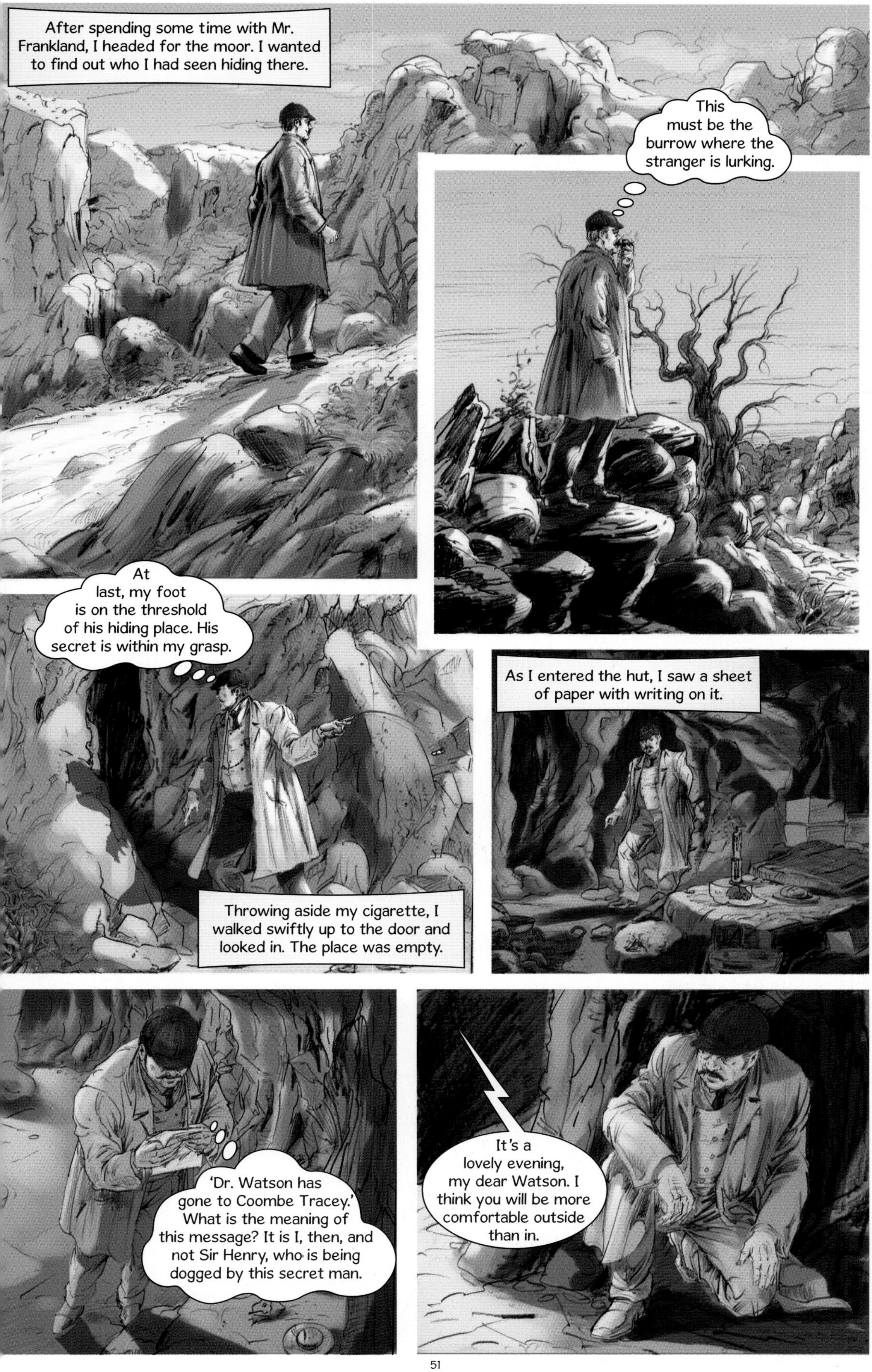

After spending some time with Mr. Frankland, I headed for the moor. I wanted to find out who I had seen hiding there.
This must be the burrow where the stranger is lurking.
At last, my foot is on the threshold of his hiding place. His secret is within my grasp.
Throwing aside my cigarette, I walked swiftly up to the door and looked in. The place was empty.
As I entered the hut, I saw a sheet of paper with writing on it.
'Dr. Watson has gone to Coombe Tracey.' What is the meaning of this message? It is I, then, and not Sir Henry, who is being dogged by this secret man.
It's a lovely evening, my dear Watson. I think you will be more comfortable outside than in.

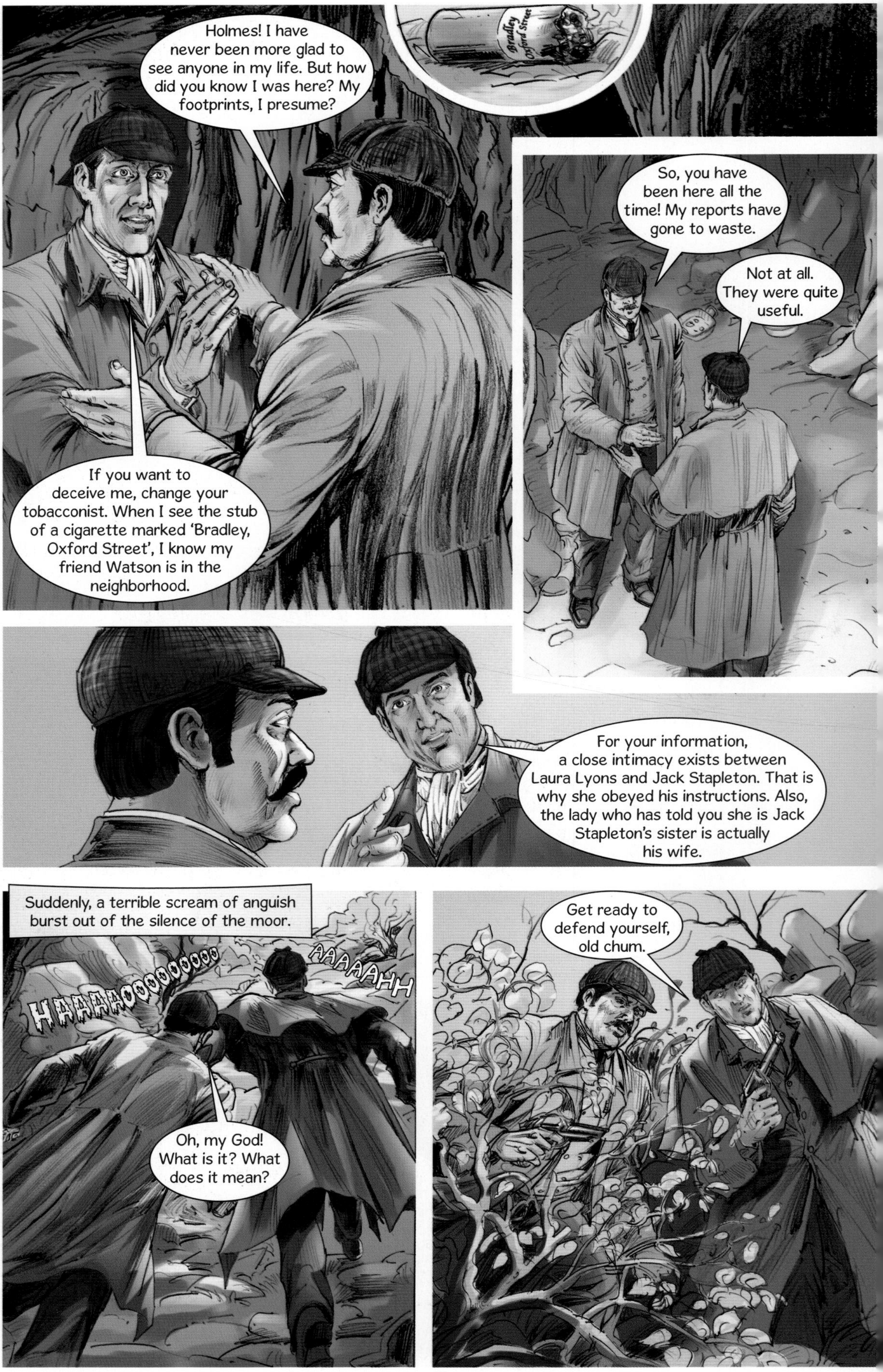

Bradley
Oxford Street
Holmes! I have never been more glad to see anyone in my life. But how did you know I was here? My footprints, I presume?
If you want to deceive me, change your tobacconist. When I see the stub of a cigarette marked 'Bradley, Oxford Street', I know my friend Watson is in the neighborhood.
So, you have been here all the time! My reports have gone to waste.
Not at all. They were quite useful.
For your information, a close intimacy exists between Laura Lyons and Jack Stapleton. That is why she obeyed his instructions. Also, the lady who has told you she is Jack Stapleton's sister is actually his wife.
Suddenly, a terrible scream of anguish burst out of the silence of the moor.
HAAAAOOOOOOOOOO
AAAAAAHH
Oh, my God! What is it? What does it mean?
Get ready to defend yourself, old chum.

The passionate and ghastly cry had come from somewhere far off on the shadowy plain. But now it burst upon our ears nearer, louder, and more urgent than before.

It came from over there. The ruins!

Hurry, Watson! The hound! My God! I hope we are not too late.

Oh, Holmes, it's Sir Henry! I will never forgive myself for leaving him to his fate.

He's been mauled to death! Definitely the work of a large animal.

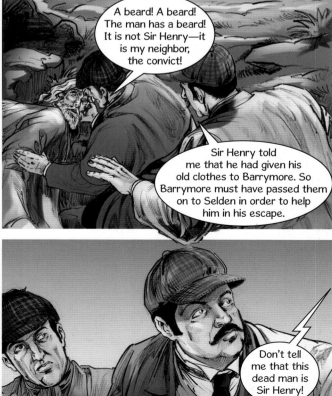

A beard! A beard! The man has a beard! It is not Sir Henry—it is my neighbor, the convict!

Sir Henry told me that he had given his old clothes to Barrymore. So Barrymore must have passed them on to Selden in order to help him in his escape.

Don't tell me that this dead man is Sir Henry!

Wait... that's **not** Sir Henry.

No. It's Selden, the convict, wearing one of Sir Henry's suits.

Th-thank goodness.

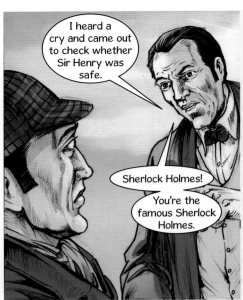

I heard a cry and came out to check whether Sir Henry was safe.

Sherlock Holmes!

You're the famous Sherlock Holmes.

I am.

Look at his throat... it looks torn. He--

The poor fellow broke his neck. He's been climbing up and down these ruins so wildly, he was bound to fall.

So that's the game you're playing, Holmes. Always concealing your true agenda.

Why were you concerned about Sir Henry in particular?

Well, I had suggested that he should come over to my place. When he didn't arrive, I got worried. I naturally became alarmed for his safety when I heard the cries upon the moor.

We should get back to Baskerville Hall and report the news to the authorities. They'll want to know the search for Selden is over.

Good day, Mr. Stapleton.

Sir Henry was more pleased than surprised to see Sherlock Holmes.

Stapleton is our villain. I am sure. And he is no fool. He had such control, even when he noticed the wrong man had been killed.

Poor Selden didn't stand a chance.

Those wounds were definitely caused by an animal. A big one, too. But where would anyone keep such a beast?

The hound's nose was fixed on you, Sir Henry. Selden was wearing your clothes.

It explains your missing shoe. Stapleton needed your scent.

I just don't understand it. Why would he want me dead?

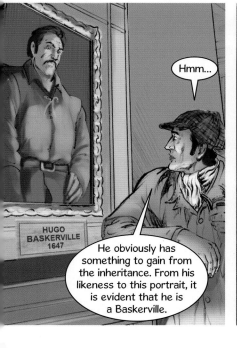

Hmm...

HUGO BASKERVILLE 1647

He obviously has something to gain from the inheritance. From his likeness to this portrait, it is evident that he is a Baskerville.

Well, I am certainly not meeting him for dinner then.

Dinner? Oh yes, I remember now. Sir Henry was showing romantic interest in Mrs. Stapleton, when Jack Stapleton caught them together. He hurled abuse at Sir Henry, but later apologized, saying that he was overprotective of his sister. He then invited Sir Henry for dinner on Friday.

Of course you are!

But he wants me dead!

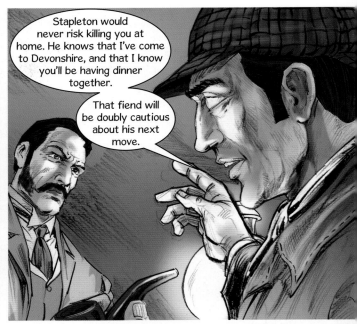

Stapleton would never risk killing you at home. He knows that I've come to Devonshire, and that I know you'll be having dinner together.

That fiend will be doubly cautious about his next move.

He won't try anything at dinner. He'll wait...

...he'll wait for you to return home, over the moor.

And we'll be watching from afar, keeping an eye out.

Precisely! Then, just at the right moment, we'll catch him in the act.

That is, of course, if you're up to it, Sir Henry.

Yes, we don't want to put you in harm's way.

Are you kidding? Let's catch that fiend!

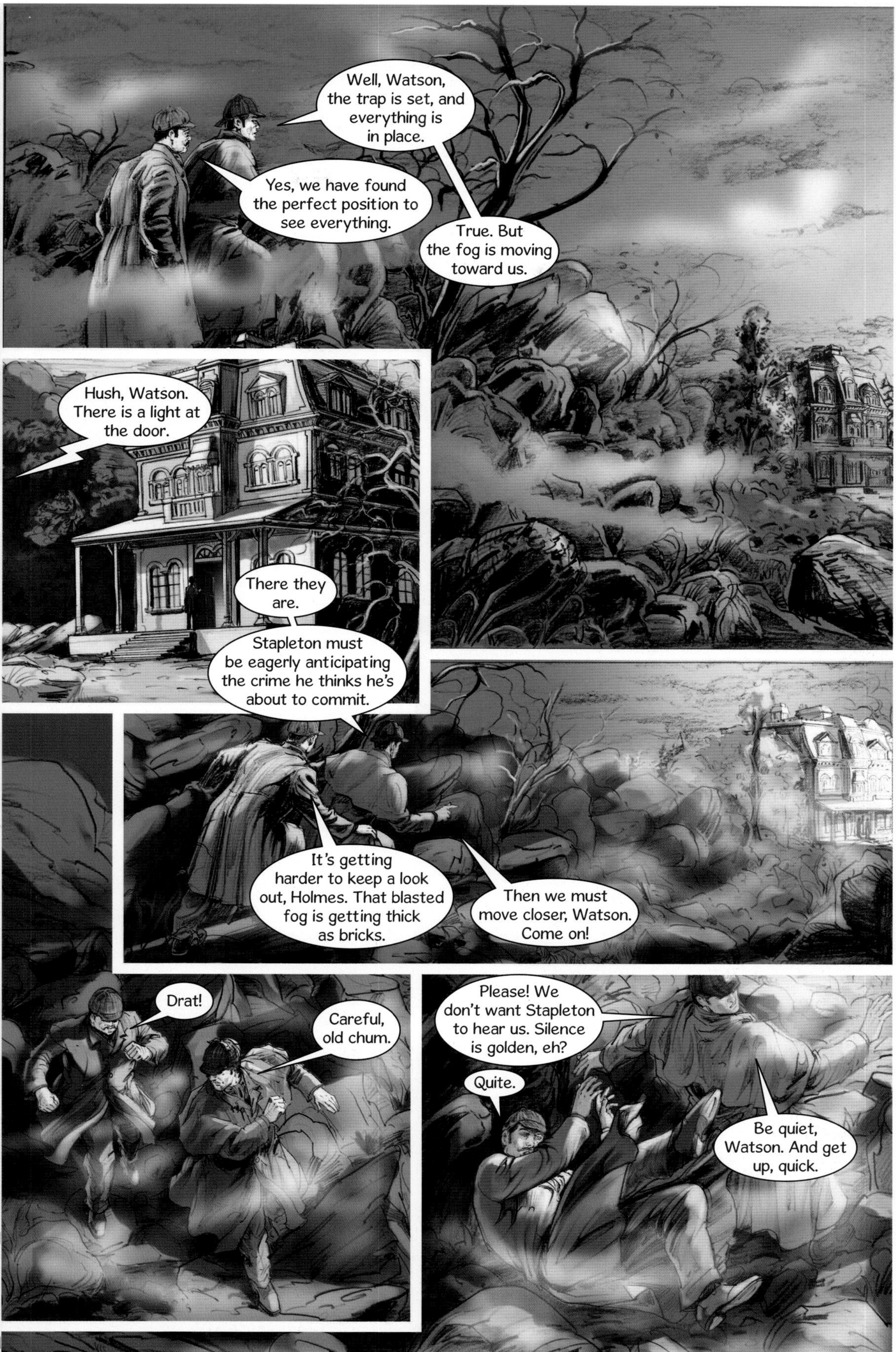
Well, Watson, the trap is set, and everything is in place.
Yes, we have found the perfect position to see everything.
True. But the fog is moving toward us.
Hush, Watson. There is a light at the door.
There they are.
Stapleton must be eagerly anticipating the crime he thinks he's about to commit.
It's getting harder to keep a look out, Holmes. That blasted fog is getting thick as bricks.
Then we must move closer, Watson. Come on!
Drat!
Careful, old chum.
Please! We don't want Stapleton to hear us. Silence is golden, eh?
Quite.
Be quiet, Watson. And get up, quick.

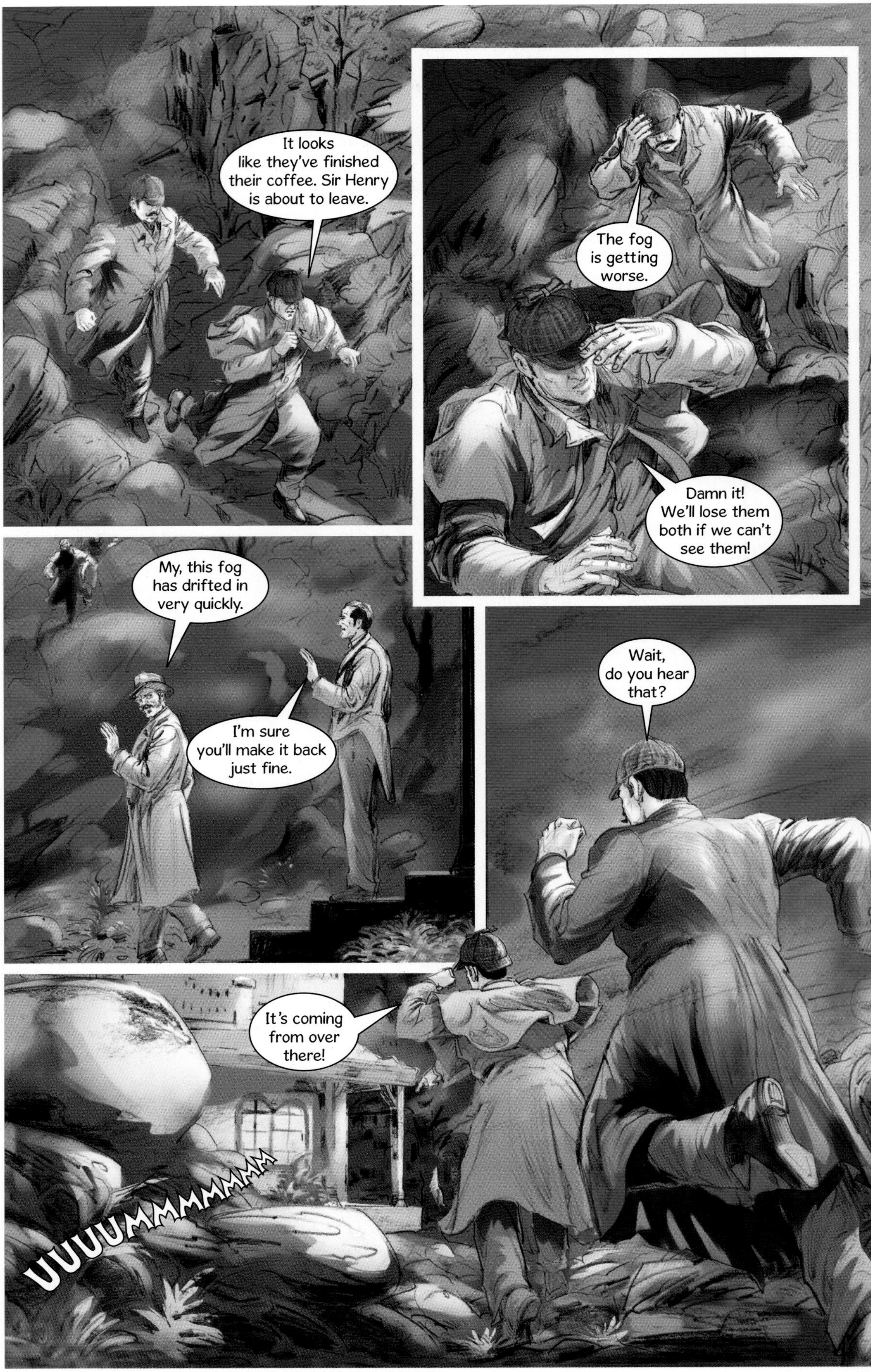
It looks like they've finished their coffee. Sir Henry is about to leave.
The fog is getting worse.
Damn it! We'll lose them both if we can't see them!
My, this fog has drifted in very quickly.
I'm sure you'll make it back just fine.
Wait, do you hear that?
It's coming from over there!
UUUUMMMMMMMM

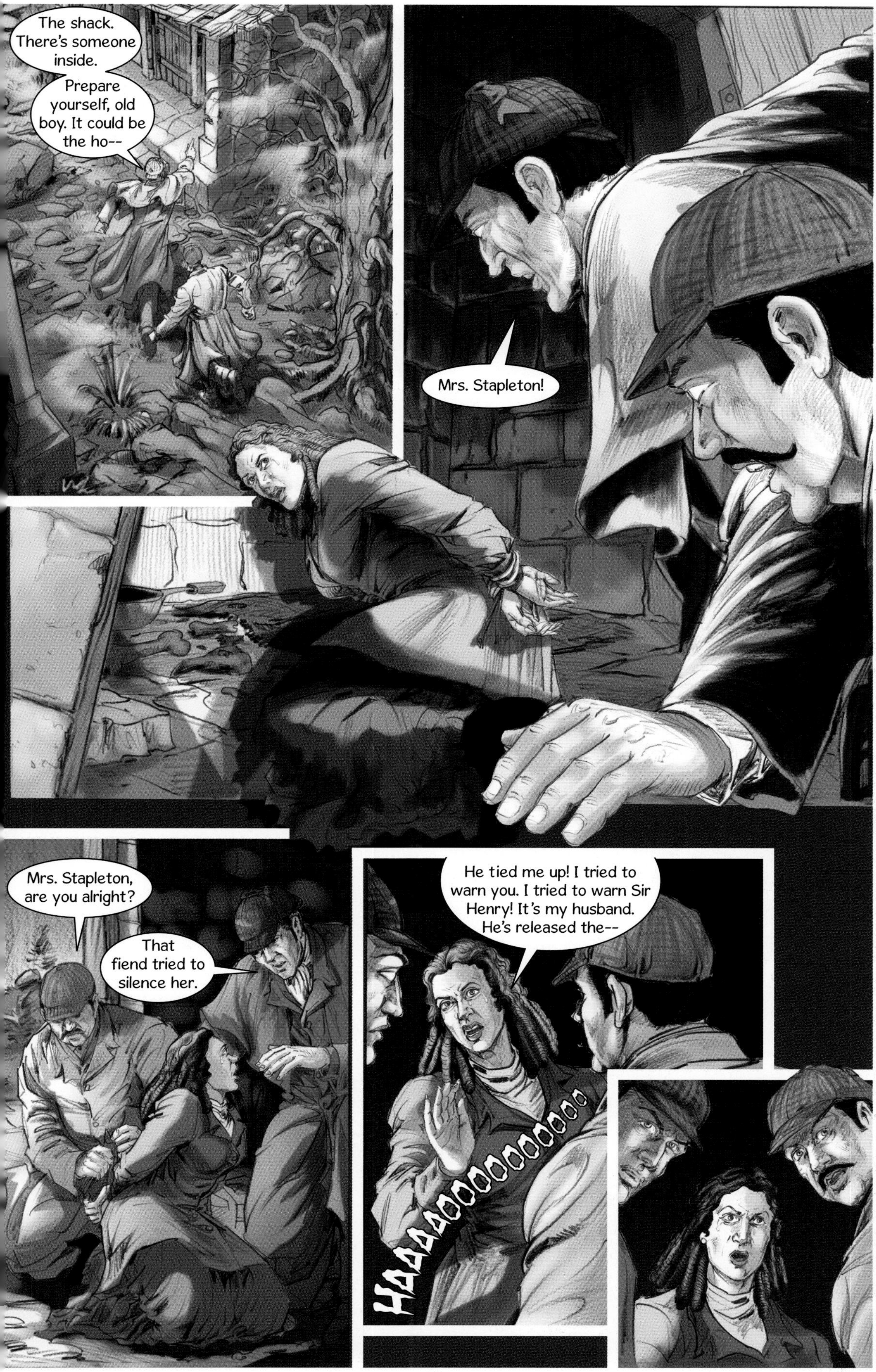
The shack. There's someone inside.
Prepare yourself, old boy. It could be the ho--
Mrs. Stapleton!
Mrs. Stapleton, are you alright?
That fiend tried to silence her.
He tied me up! I tried to warn you. I tried to warn Sir Henry! It's my husband. He's released the--
HAAAOOOOOOOOOOO

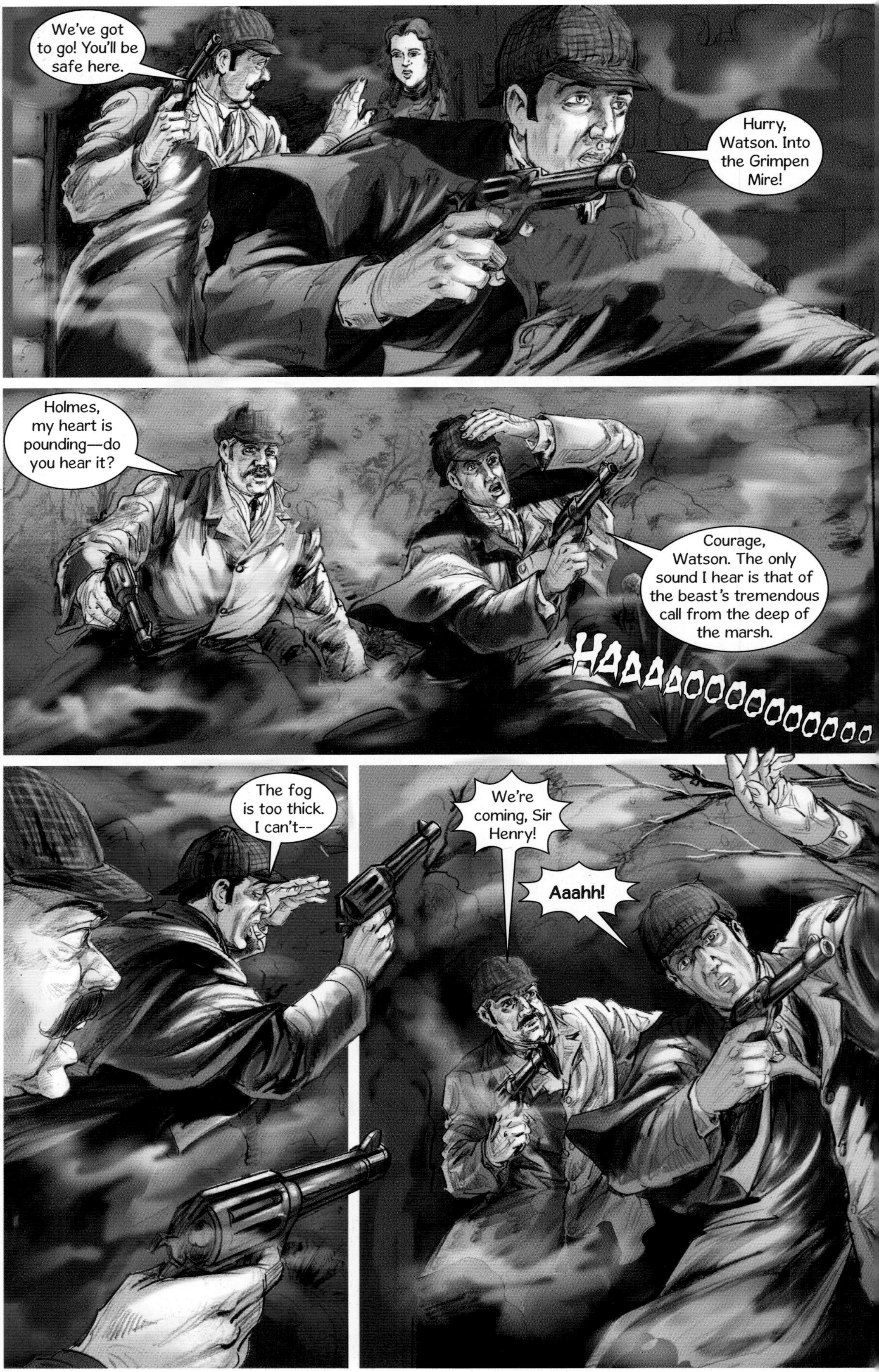
We've got to go! You'll be safe here.
Hurry, Watson. Into the Grimpen Mire!
Holmes, my heart is pounding—do you hear it?
Courage, Watson. The only sound I hear is that of the beast's tremendous call from the deep of the marsh.
HAAAAOOOOOOOOOO
The fog is too thick. I can't--
We're coming, Sir Henry!
Aaahh!

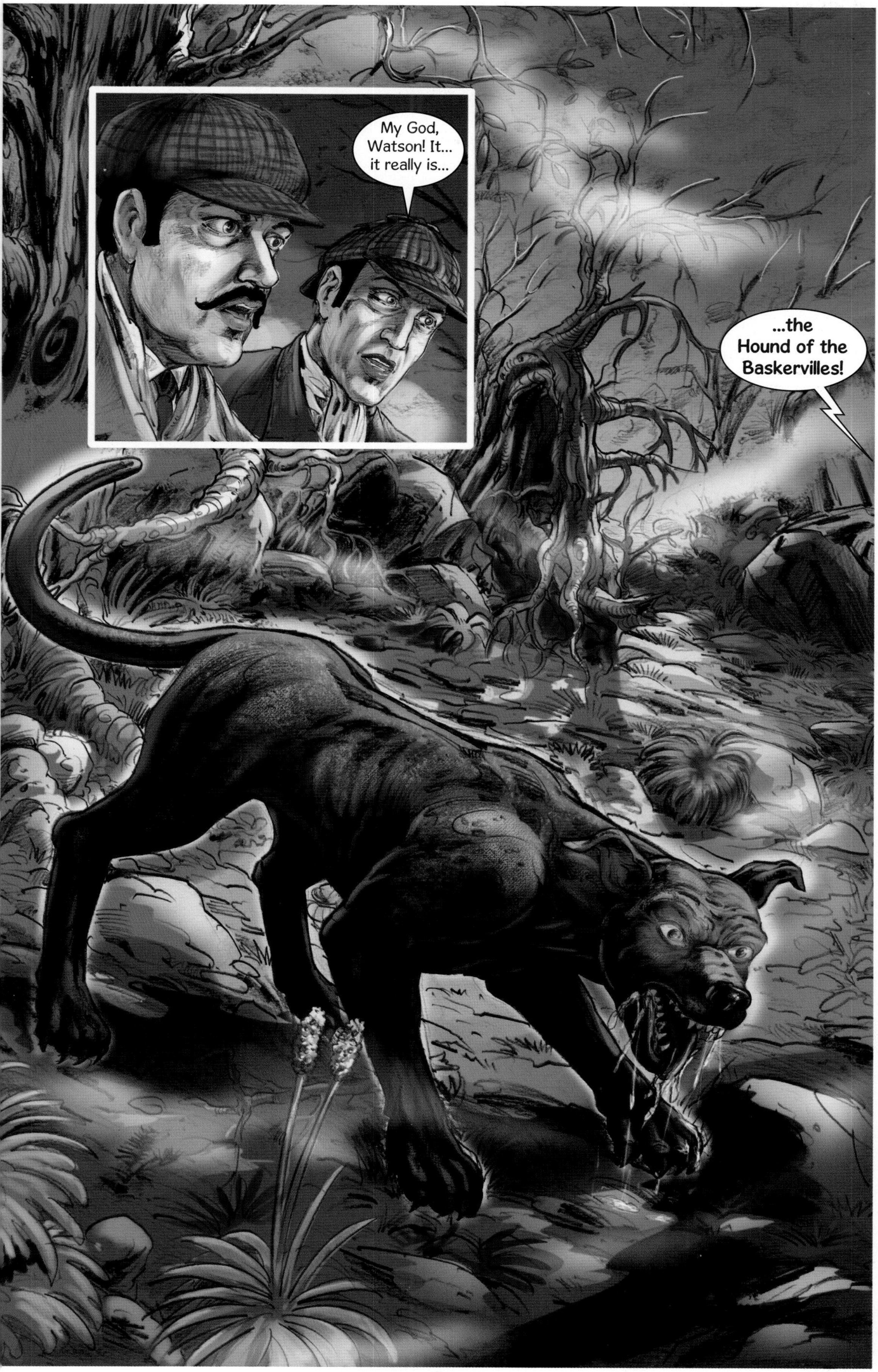
My God, Watson! It... it really is...
...the Hound of the Baskervilles!

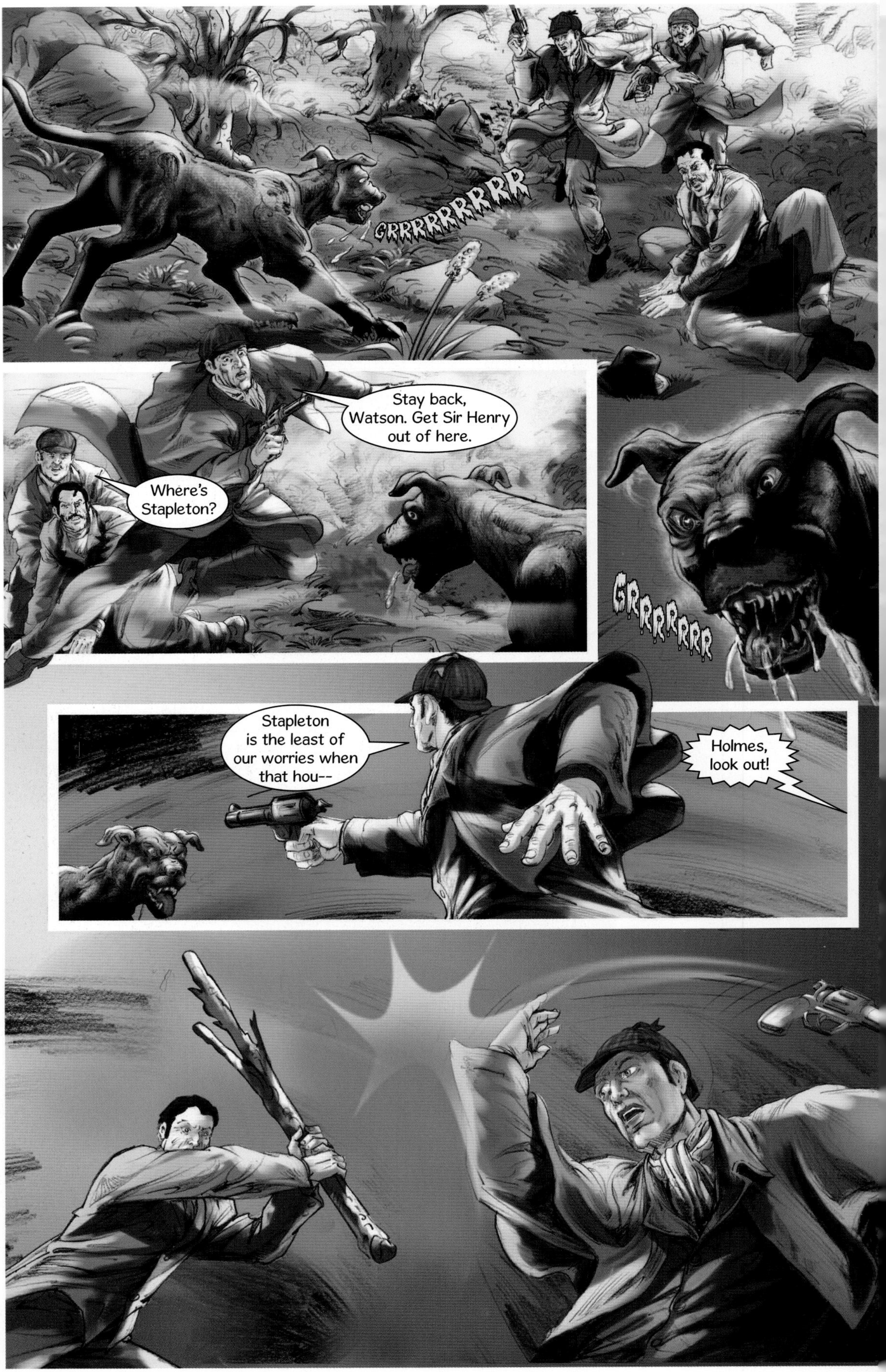
GRRRRRRRRR
Stay back, Watson. Get Sir Henry out of here.
Where's Stapleton?
GRRRRRRR
Stapleton is the least of our worries when that hou--
Holmes, look out!

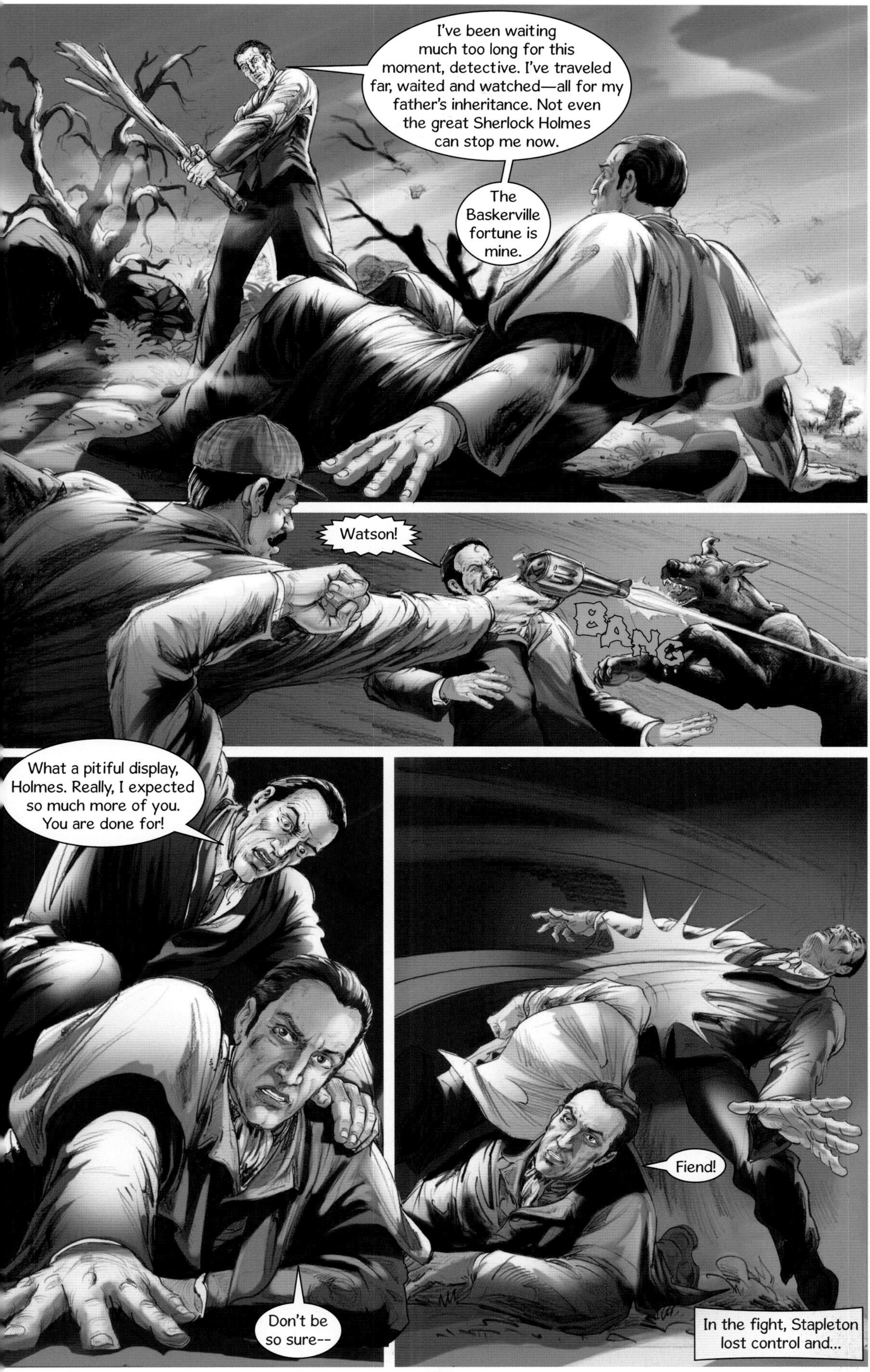
I've been waiting much too long for this moment, detective. I've traveled far, waited and watched—all for my father's inheritance. Not even the great Sherlock Holmes can stop me now.
The Baskerville fortune is mine.
Watson!
BANG
What a pitiful display, Holmes. Really, I expected so much more of you. You are done for!
Don't be so sure--
Fiend!
In the fight, Stapleton lost control and...

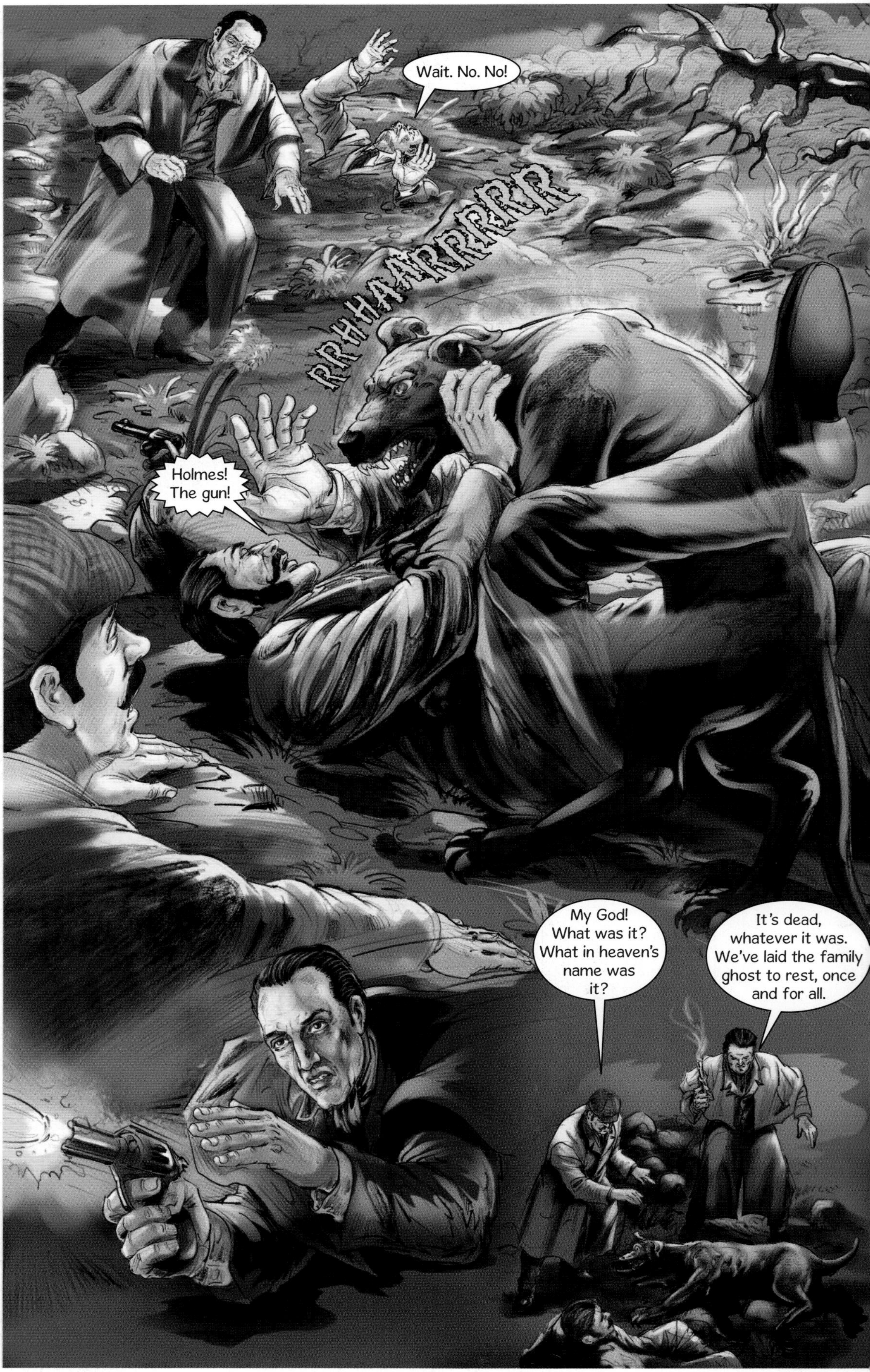
Wait. No. No!
RRHHAARRRRR
Holmes! The gun!
My God! What was it? What in heaven's name was it?
It's dead, whatever it was. We've laid the family ghost to rest, once and for all.

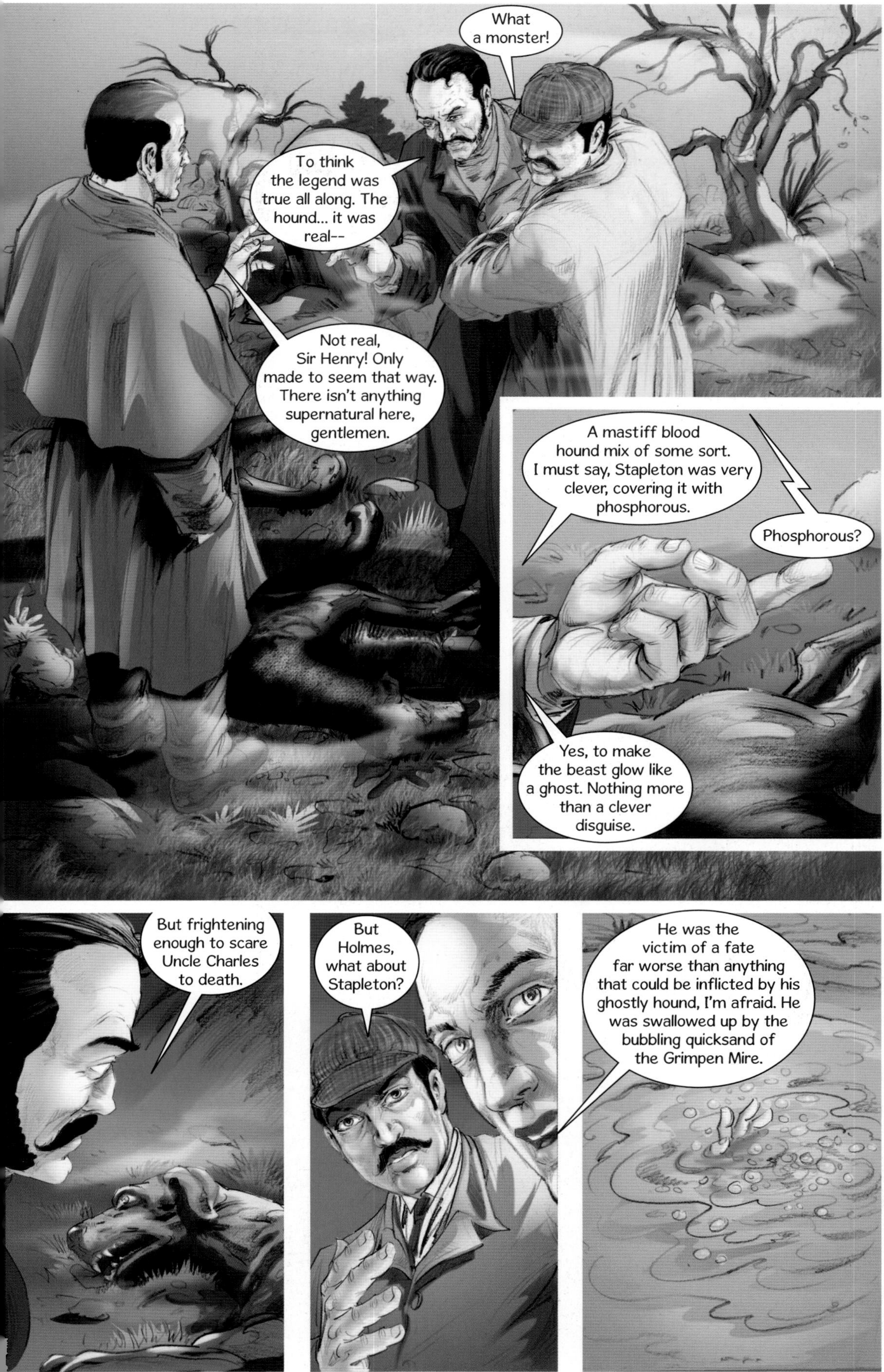
What a monster!
To think the legend was true all along. The hound... it was real--
Not real, Sir Henry! Only made to seem that way. There isn't anything supernatural here, gentlemen.
A mastiff blood hound mix of some sort. I must say, Stapleton was very clever, covering it with phosphorous.
Phosphorous?
Yes, to make the beast glow like a ghost. Nothing more than a clever disguise.
But frightening enough to scare Uncle Charles to death.
But Holmes, what about Stapleton?
He was the victim of a fate far worse than anything that could be inflicted by his ghostly hound, I'm afraid. He was swallowed up by the bubbling quicksand of the Grimpen Mire.

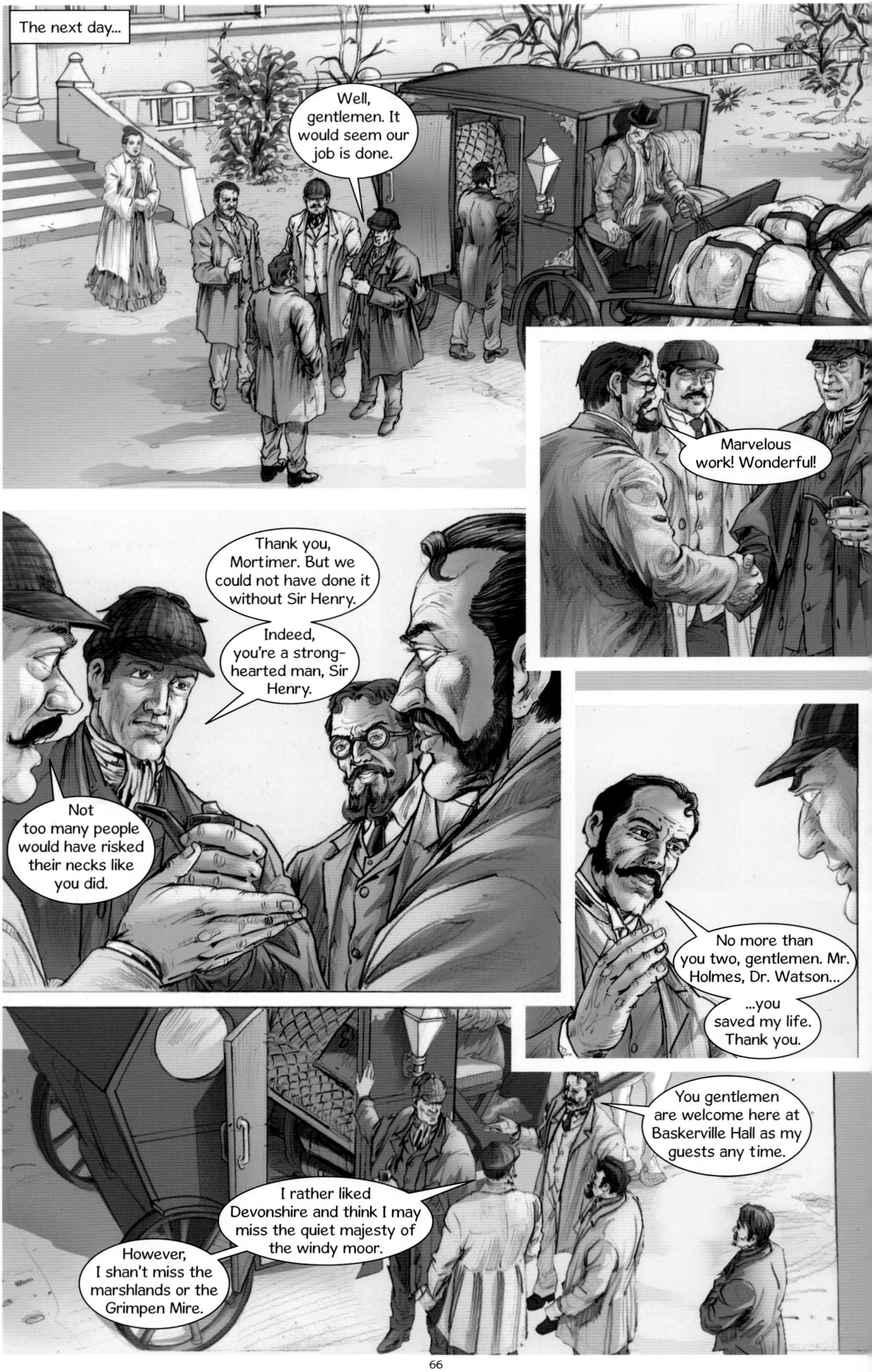
The next day...
Well, gentlemen. It would seem our job is done.
Marvelous work! Wonderful!
Thank you, Mortimer. But we could not have done it without Sir Henry.
Indeed, you're a strong-hearted man, Sir Henry.
Not too many people would have risked their necks like you did.
No more than you two, gentlemen. Mr. Holmes, Dr. Watson...
...you saved my life. Thank you.
You gentlemen are welcome here at Baskerville Hall as my guests any time.
I rather liked Devonshire and think I may miss the quiet majesty of the windy moor.
However, I shan't miss the marshlands or the Grimpen Mire.

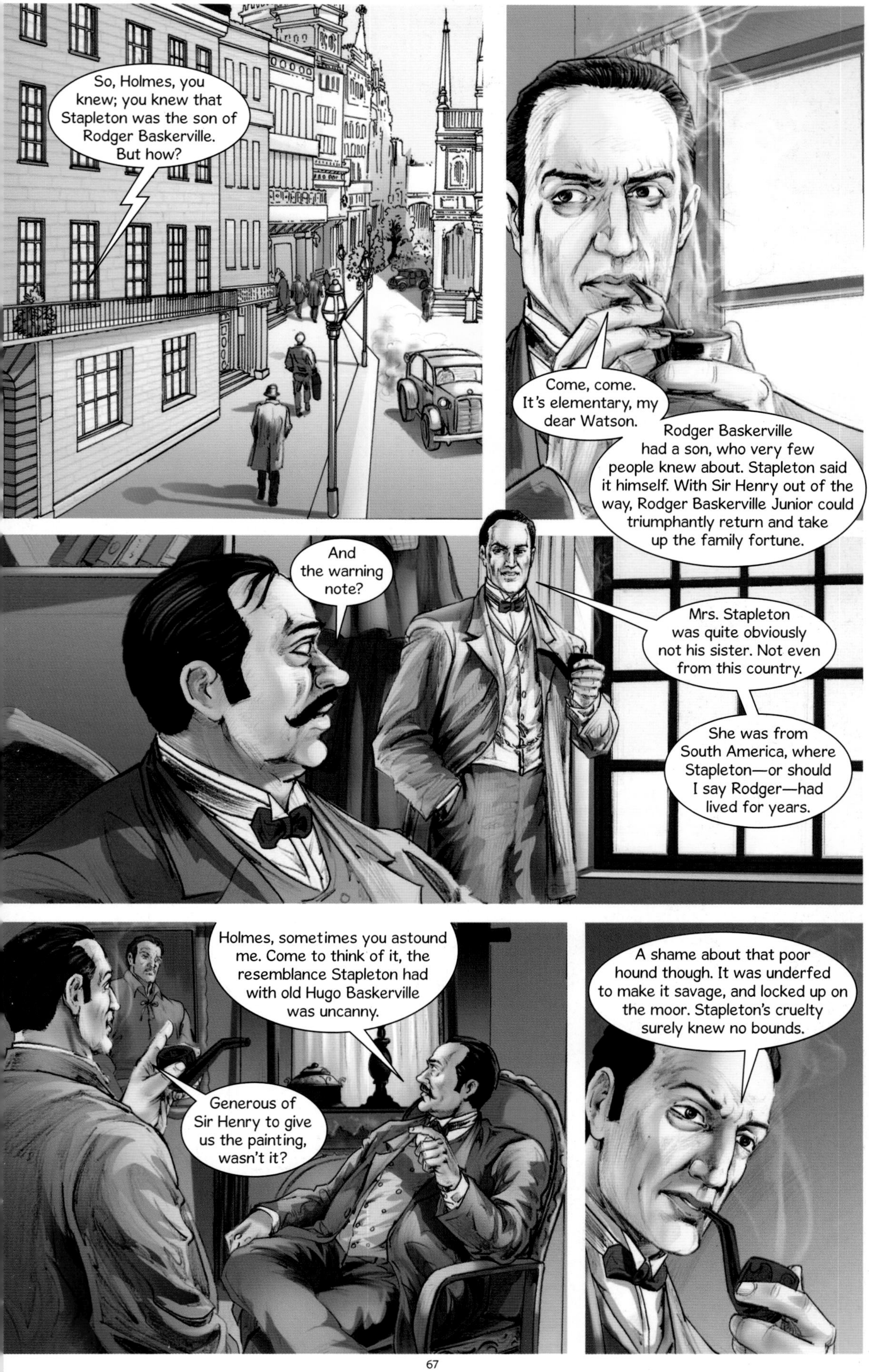
So, Holmes, you knew; you knew that Stapleton was the son of Rodger Baskerville. But how?
Come, come. It's elementary, my dear Watson.
Rodger Baskerville had a son, who very few people knew about. Stapleton said it himself. With Sir Henry out of the way, Rodger Baskerville Junior could triumphantly return and take up the family fortune.
And the warning note?
Mrs. Stapleton was quite obviously not his sister. Not even from this country.
She was from South America, where Stapleton—or should I say Rodger—had lived for years.
Holmes, sometimes you astound me. Come to think of it, the resemblance Stapleton had with old Hugo Baskerville was uncanny.
Generous of Sir Henry to give us the painting, wasn't it?
A shame about that poor hound though. It was underfed to make it savage, and locked up on the moor. Stapleton's cruelty surely knew no bounds.

COLLECTIBLE CANINES

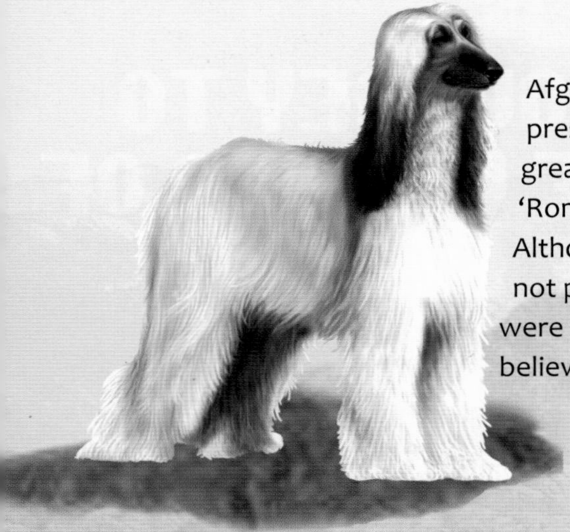

AFGHAN HOUND

Afghan hounds, as their name suggests, originated in present-day Afghanistan thousands of years ago. A great favorite at dog shows, they are often called the 'Roman Nose' because of their long, straight muzzle. Although very athletic and gentle by nature, they are not particularly friendly creatures. In olden times, they were herders and hunters. Strangely, though, they are believed to be the dumbest of all dogs!

Snuppy, the first cloned dog in the world, was an Afghan hound.

NEWFOUNDLAND

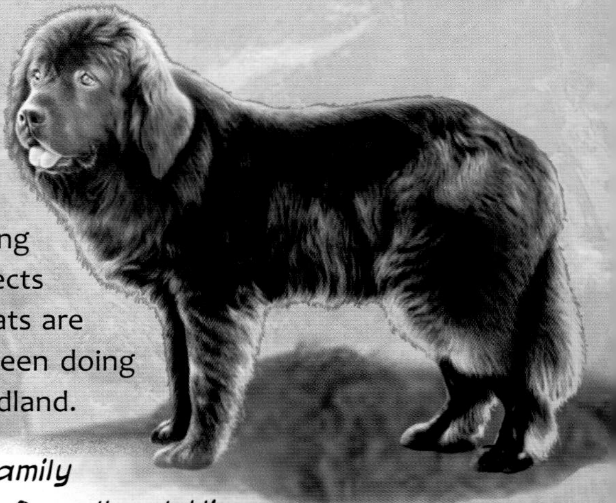

These dogs are bear-like and extremely friendly. Interestingly, Newfoundlands, or Newfies as they are sometimes called, have webbed feet and waterproof coats, so it's not surprising that they simply love anything to do with water. Lifesaving, retrieving objects thrown into the water and even towing boats are all great fun for them. They can often be seen doing such things in their land of origin—Newfoundland.

Nana, the pet dog of the Darling family in J. M. Barrie's Peter Pan, is a Newfoundland. His character was based on the author's dog, Porthos.

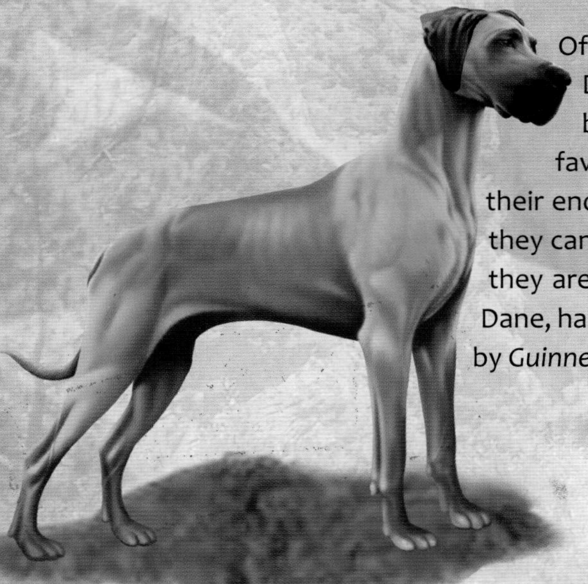

GREAT DANE

Often called the 'Apollo of Dogdom', Great Danes are very tall dogs with a booming bark. Adept at hunting, they were a great favorite of the nobility of the past. Despite their enormous size (standing on their hind legs, they can easily look a six-foot person in the eye), they are gentle giants. Gibson, a 42.2-inch Great Dane, has been named the tallest dog in the world by Guinness World Records!

Scooby Doo, the famous cartoon character, is a Great Dane.

DID YOU KNOW?

- The smallest dog in the world is the Chihuahua.
- The heaviest dog in the world is the Old English Mastiff.
- The fastest dog in the world is the Greyhound.

DID YOU KNOW?

- The Chow is a breed that has a jet black tongue.
- Dogs sweat through the pads of their feet.
- The Basenji is a called the 'Voiceless Dog' because it cannot bark.

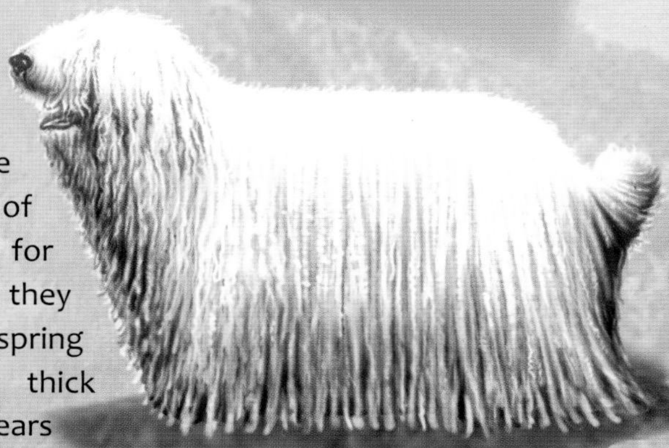

KOMONDOR

A huge mop on four legs. That's exactly what Komondors look like! They are very common in Hungary, their land of origin, and are bred as guard dogs for sheep. They are perfect for this job, as they can blend in easily with the sheep and spring surprise attacks on predators. Their thick protective coat helps them to fight bears and wolves! At the same time, they are quiet dogs at home, and are very protective of their owners.

Komondors were almost wiped out in Hungary during World War II. The invading German soldiers had to kill the fierce dogs in order to get to the farms and houses they were guarding!

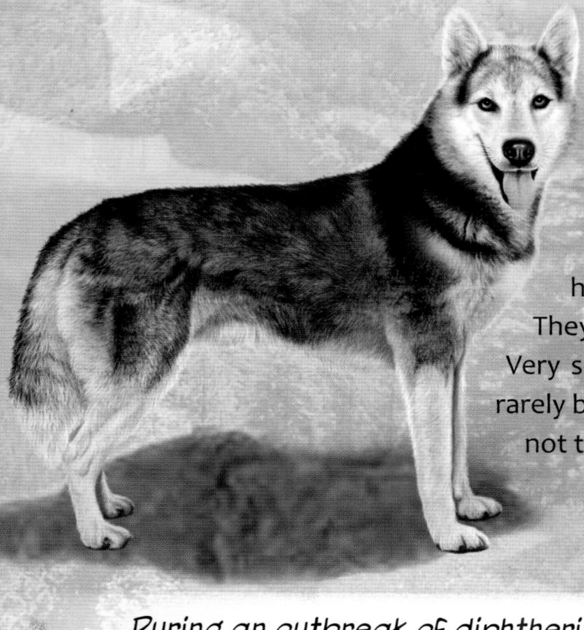

SIBERIAN HUSKY

The Chukchi people of Siberia depended on Siberian Huskies to survive in earlier days. These strong dogs pulled sleds and herded livestock in freezing conditions. They are sledge and cart racing champions. Very sociable, they hate being left alone. They rarely bark, but let out howls like wolves, and are not the best guard dogs.

During an outbreak of diphtheria in 1925, it was a team of Siberian Huskies that delivered a much-needed serum to the isolated town of Nome in Alaska.

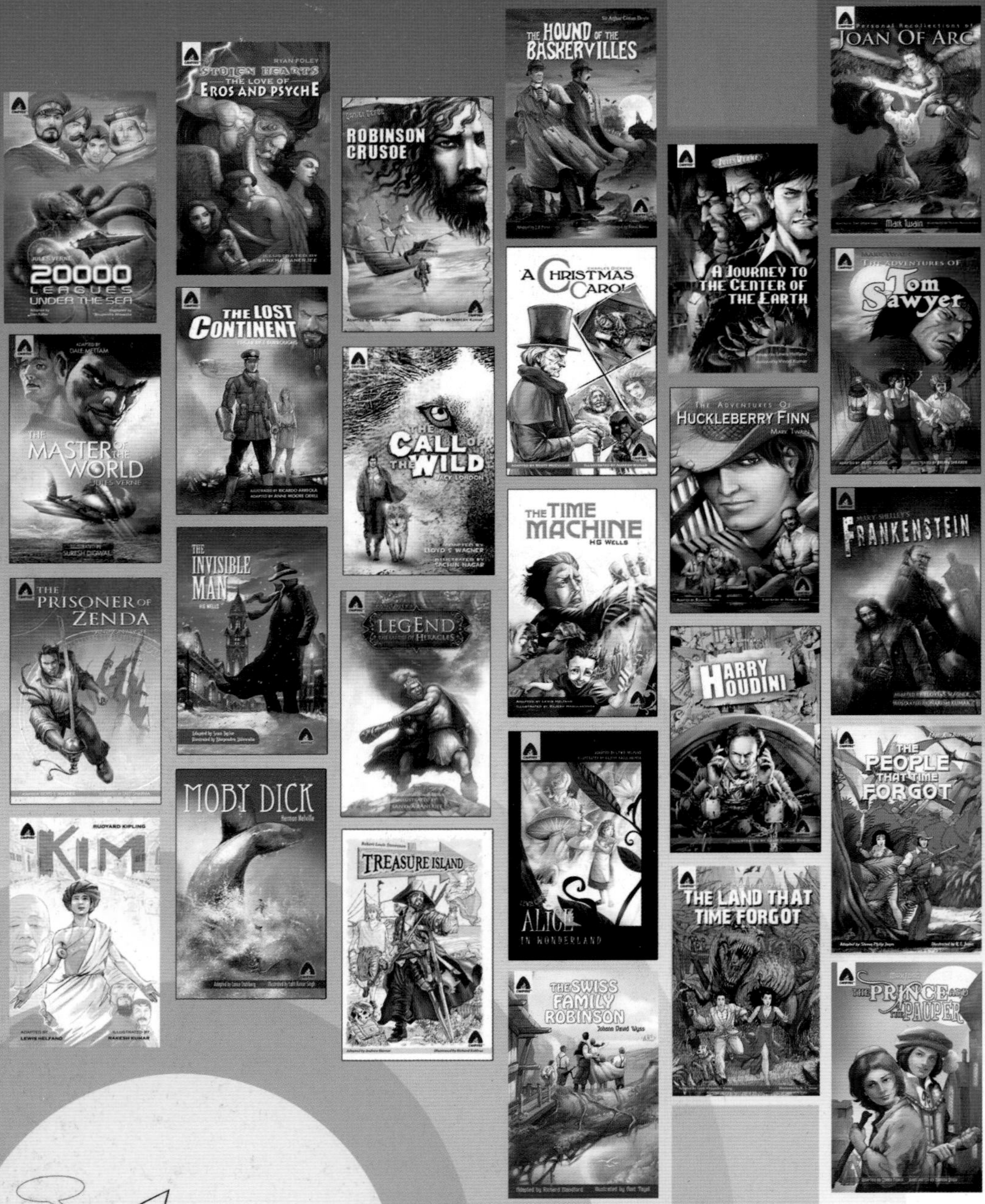
20000 LEAGUES UNDER THE SEA
STOLEN HEARTS THE LOVE OF EROS AND PSYCHE
ROBINSON CRUSOE
THE HOUND OF THE BASKERVILLES
JOAN OF ARC
A JOURNEY TO THE CENTER OF THE EARTH
THE MASTER OF THE WORLD
THE LOST CONTINENT
THE CALL OF THE WILD
A CHRISTMAS CAROL
THE ADVENTURES OF Tom Sawyer
THE ADVENTURES OF HUCKLEBERRY FINN
THE TIME MACHINE
FRANKENSTEIN
THE PRISONER OF ZENDA
THE INVISIBLE MAN
LEGEND THE LABOURS OF HERACLES
HARRY HOUDINI
THE PEOPLE THAT TIME FORGOT
KIM
MOBY DICK
TREASURE ISLAND
ALICE IN WONDERLAND
THE LAND THAT TIME FORGOT
THE SWISS FAMILY ROBINSON
THE PRINCE AND THE PAUPER